"How do you want to spend *your* life, *Reuben*?" The emphasis on his name was a kind of dare. "If you don't watch out," she said, "it just slips through your fingers."

Come on, how old could she be? Nineteen? Twenty?

Then another quick change. She got up and crossed the room and trailed languid fingers along his cheek. "Ah, Reuben-Reuben."

He grabbed her wrist. "What's going on, Zoe?"

The exotic face lost its composure. Her eyes widened with fright. Her chin trembled. "Let me go!" she cried.

Startled, he let her go.

"I'm sorry," she whispered, rubbing her wrist though he was sure he couldn't have hurt her. "It's just—I needed company because I woke up terrified. . . ."

By Cecil Dawkins
Published by Ivy Books:

THE SANTA FE REMBRANDT
CLAY DANCERS
RARE EARTH
TURTLE TRUTHS

TURTLE TRUTHS

Cecil Dawkins

IVY BOOKS • NEW YORK

An Ivy Book
Published by Ballantine Books
Copyright © 1997 by Cecil Dawkins

All rights reserved under International and Pan-American Copyright Conventions. Published in the United States by Ballantine Books, a division of Random House, Inc., New York, and simultaneously in Canada by Random House of Canada Limited, Toronto.

http://www.randomhouse.com

Library of Congress Catalog Card Number: 97-92211

ISBN 0-8041-1433-1

Manufactured in the United States of America

First Edition: November 1997

10 9 8 7 6 5 4 3 2 1

1

The sky was milky blue with thinning mare's tails. Plenty of wind up there, but jogging along earthbound, Reuben was sweating. Between rock formations off to his left the highway now and then appeared, looped over the landscape like that ribbon road in the Georgia O'Keefe painting. The outback north of Santa Fe offered up to his painter's eye pink sandstone formations like something from Karnak or the Valley of Kings. Creatures. Heads of big birds all facing the same direction. Stacks of extinct weapons leaning against the cliffs, or friezes on some Moorish temple of armies wearing hats like bagels.

The scenery could be distracting, which was the case when he rounded a sandstone knob and stumbled upon, almost literally, the man lying across the trail.

Recognition was instant. He was older, that bright wing of hair had thinned, and the forehead was ridged with undeniable middle age, but the man on the ground, who lifted a small apologetic smile as if to say he was sorry to be such an inconvenience, was Anthony Quayle, acclaimed and beknighted star of stage and screen.

He struggled to rise but fell back clutching his chest.

Reuben leapt forward and caught him before his head touched the ground.

His involvement with the beautiful people happened that simply, though he thought it complicated. But that only reflects how he viewed his own life compared to other people's.

2

In Turtle Bay on Jamaica's north shore, Matilde watched with disapproval the wedding taking place in the bougainvillea arbor. "No good will come-ah dis happening," she said to the houseboy.

But the houseboy ignored her and summoned the caterer. "Comb-yah, mahn."

Matilde muttered under her breath. She was from Montego Bay and new to the plantation, grudgingly helping out her great-aunt Boll, whose hip refused to mend.

Her refreshment cart was set under the giant banyan tree, a forest in itself, which like a patient python was slowly swallowing a wrought-iron garden bench. All that remained to the tree's digestion was the lower shin of one garlanded wrought-iron leg.

"Sumaddy here creh-zy," she said to the houseboy's back.

"Mine yuh mout'," he muttered, moving with his tray toward the wedding guests in the sunny garden.

But Matilde would not be silenced. "She ancien' enough to be the bwai's gret-grandma and cripple to boot."

The garden, alive with red and yellow hibiscus, creamy frangipani, magenta bougainvillea, and tree-climbing

3

orchids, undulated over a green hill above the bay. Below was the beach, and beyond, ridged by a breeze into corrugated metal under the midday sun, the Caribbean waters rolled to the horizon.

Presently the ceremony drew to a close, and the bridegroom trundled the bride's wheelchair along the walk toward the refreshments. In high church vestments, the clergyman, as dark as Jamaican coffee, gripped his prayer book with an air of finality and followed at a distance.

From a branch of the banyan tree the bride's scarlet macaw watched the approach. The parrot had spiraled up the plump trunk in the pale light of dawn to perch there with his friend the gray lori, now sleeping sweetly under the protection of the macaw's flaming wing. As a fledgling, the parrot had been a gift to the bride from her father on her tenth birthday, but now he was seventy-five years old, he had seen much, and he was bored and rich. For the life span of a parrot is long, and his mistress had set up a trust fund in his name at a bank in Montego Bay.

The old bride lifted a blue-veined hand and greeted the guests converging upon the rum punch in a crystal bowl of floating hibiscus.

Matilde, outraged by the costly layers of makeup on the old bride's face, refused to look. She filled the goblets with a silver ladle and watched the hands—white, and black, and every shade between—reach for the crystal stems.

The macaw puffed out his breast and voiced his disapproval of the goings-on. His raucous cry caused a flock of songbirds to rise in alarm from the upper branches of the banyan tree. But few of the wedding guests glanced up at the familiar racket or the flight against the sky, though the gray lori sidestepped along the limb to distance herself from her noisy protector. The macaw, however, moved instantly after her and trapped her again beneath his wing.

"So, Charlotte," the old deaf judge bellowed, leaning over the bride in her wheelchair, "you're off on a wedding trip." He rocked back in a self-satisfied way on the heels of his pumps, holding the punch glass daintily atop the vast expanse of his belly.

"Don't shout at me, old man," the bride said. "You're the one deaf, not I."

"We are going to the States," the bridegroom said softly.

"First to Baltimore for my eighty-thousand-mile checkup!" She laughed. "And then to New Mexico."

"Mexico, is it!" shouted the judge. "As a young man I once visited the Mexican capital."

The bride said impatiently, "You get deafer by the day, old man. The only capital we'll visit is Santa Fe."

The doctor, as gray as the lori, murmured, "Tut-tut, I've warned you against that nonsense, Charlotte. The altitude . . . Now promise you won't neglect your medications."

The bride chuckled. "I plan to outlive you all."

But the doctor said sternly to the bridegroom, "See she behaves herself, Simon."

The bride tapped her cane on the leg of her handsome mahogany-colored groom in his crimson vest and navy suit. "Come along, Simon. We must be going."

The young man set down his plate of refreshments half-eaten and sprang behind the old lady's chair, and Matilde commented scornfully under her breath. "Creh-zy, creh-zy."

The bride waved a jeweled hand on an arm where the

flesh melted like candle wax, and the bridegroom rolled her up the path toward the plantation house where a driver arranged luggage in the trunk of a black Rolls brougham and Jane Boll, the housekeeper, watched from the upper verandah, shaking her head at this new foolishness.

With a bad-tempered shriek the macaw dropped from the banyan tree to alight on the path behind the wedding pair. The guests all watched the curious procession make its slow way up the hill—old bride, young groom, and the grumbling parrot waddling after them with lazy wings.

3

The bridegroom had spent the last night of his bachelorhood drinking with his friend Eugene aboard the pirate ship anchored in the bay. Eugene was the master of work, in charge of overhauling the centuries-old sailing vessel—to be used, he had heard, as a tourist attraction over there in Cuba, ninety miles to the north across the Gulf. Eugene was also the watchman and lived on board, sleeping on deck these warm tropical nights, lulled by the gentle motion of the sea.

Lolling back on a hatch cover, he squeezed a lime into his rum Coke. "You really gone do this thing, mahn?"

Simon stirred his drink with his finger. "Haven't I said it, bruh?" Thanks to Dame Charlotte, he was Oxford educated, but at home he lapsed into Jamaica talk.

Reggae came from the resort hotel on one horn of the half-moon bay. Even at this late hour bathing couples were silhouetted by the colored lights playing over the fake waterfall plunging, soundlessly at this distance, into the swimming pool. At the other point of the horn, the cruise ship that had docked at midnight glittered in silent splendor, its reflected tiers of lights multiplied in the still waters of Turtle Bay.

Eugene said, "Gabriel say he be coming."

"He won't come. Gabriel drunk by now. He cyain hold his Dragon Stout."

"Sometime Gabriel he jook me."

"These days he drunk wid Jah," Simon said.

"I think he put that on."

Simon sipped his rum while reggae gave way to calypso, and with a certain irony Eugene repeated the words. "Come to Jamaica where de rum come from . . . de rum come from . . . de rum come from."

The pirate ship had made the trip home from England on the deck of a tanker, an indignity for a vessel that once harassed Spanish galleons bound for Spain with hulls full of silver and gold. Already it had appeared in American films, an industry Jamaica encouraged. In one of them, Eugene himself swung from the rigging in striped jersey and white duck trousers ripped off at the knee, sporting a brace of pistols in his belt and one gold hoop earring, while in the foreground, being rowed out in the ship's boat, the star—in top hat and high cravat and swallowtail coat—stood resolutely gazing out to sea.

Something slapped the water like a big fish jumping. They turned to watch a swimmer stroke powerfully toward them, sending a rain of phosphorescence into the dark.

"Hey, mahn," Eugene called over the water. And low to Simon, "He here now."

The swimmer rose over the gunnels like a black Poseidon, large and naked and glistening in the dim yellow light of the overhead lantern. He shook himself vigorously, raining a squall down on Simon and Eugene from his wild dreadlocks, laughing when they ducked.

Eugene tossed him a limp towel.

"How come have you left the ruinate?" Simon asked.

His giant brother seldom walked out of the lushness of the mountain, where the forest had taken over the abandoned fields of once rich plantations.

The newcomer said in a sibilant whisper, "Jah sent me to look after you, bredda."

Simon was never sure if Gabriel believed himself an emissary of the divine, or if this were one more of the disguises with which he confronted the outside world. Beyond the Cockpits and the mountain, with his size and his poor unfinished face, Gabriel was not at home.

He bent and placed his large hands tenderly on either side of Simon's head and whispered breathily, "I could tek you in han', bwai, and crush alla that fine edu-*ceh*-shun out of you."

Simon calmly shoved Gabriel's hands aside. Eugene, bent over the ship's rail, opted for nonparticipation. He raised a bucket on a rope and sloshed salt water across the deck where earlier he had cleaned a fish.

"Why you no dread your hair," Gabriel whispered, "if you one of us? Half of you one a them." Muscles bulging in the lantern light, he lifted his slender brother by his shirtfront. "What they ever done but mek us slehves?"

"Get a grip, Gabriel," Simon said softly.

But his brother hissed, "What we got? We tek back the ruinate, we got the Cockpits"—the limestone knob-and-valley mountain land pitted with caves into the island's viscera—"but we still slehves. Sweep they floors, wait they tables, rock they babbies, they t'row us change. 'T'ank you, t'ank you' "—bobbing servilely, slinging salt droplets from his dreadlocks into Simon's face. "Before long they'll want all we got. They come with they money, poah folks say gimme-gimme, and tek they paypah, and run to the city to live in a dungle and drink

ourselves dead on rum while they say, 'Poah black
peoples got no hambition.' "

Simon marveled as always that Gabriel no longer
whispered and hissed but grew eloquent in his passion.

"But I got hambition. Hambition to live my way, ina
house made wid my hands, ina garden wid coupl'a chickens and goats, and pickneys running nekit and happy. No
condo high-rises, no big cyahs. What we want widdim?
What good it do?"

He released Simon, flinging him back against the ship's
rail. "You don' like us, bruh, because we black and dumb
and ugly, and you edu-*ceh*-ted and light and pritty!"

Simon pulled himself up and said softly, "No, those
are the reasons you don't like me, bruh."

Eugene at the rail said, "What you want, Gabe?"

Gabriel turned away from the lantern light and, with
his hands wide at his sides on the ship's rail, leaned over
the dark water. "I stop by the pleh-ce looking for Simon.
She say she want him, *now*." He smiled contemptuously.
"She twitch your string, you better run."

Simon downed the last of his rum and, ignoring the sly
deprecating smiles, leapt over the side of the pirate ship
and landed on the plywood roof of his uncle's glass-
bottom boat that by day took tourists out to the reef to see
the tropical fish, and sometimes by night delivered bales
of Rasta grass beyond the reef to a waiting powerboat.

Eugene and Gabriel listened while the motor sputtered
to life. As the small boat putted in toward the deserted
beach, the preserve of tourists, fenced off and its gates
locked at night against locals, Eugene said, "Tomorrow
he belong to her lock, stock, an' barrel, what she want
widdim tonight?"

Gabriel reached into Eugene's Styrofoam cooler and

popped a beer. He had no use for rum. He called it "tourist piss." He whispered breathily from beyond reach of the lantern, protecting his deformity from the light, "He belong to her like a thing. She do widdim whatever."

Eugene shrugged. He liked the rum. He liked the tourists. Most of them tipped handsomely. "Tomorrow he go chack to Miami an' who knows where else," he said with envy. But then he added, "Never mind, it will all work out. Simon do right by us."

Simon was Eugene's friend from childhood, but now it was Gabriel who assumed his allegiance, a strange and disturbing turn of events. He drew in a breath of the salt night air, longing to escape to carefree days of rum and girls on the beaches.

But Gabriel loomed up beside him in the dark. "Better a sleh-ve stripping cane than some animal outside his pleh-ce. Gotchoo some ganja, mahn?"

Eugene took a pipe and a drawstring pouch from his pocket and passed them to Gabriel, and watched him fish out the little rocks of hash with his fingers and stack the bowl. Gabriel called himself a Maroon and spent a lot of time up in Trelawny Parish, just like those old escaped slaves holed up in their towns in the hills, chasing wild pigs for jerk meat, those runaways who in the old days banded together up there in the Cockpit Country and terrified white plantation owners.

The Maroons might have been ancestors to them all, but, Eugene argued silently, times have changed, though Gabriel kept to himself too much to know it. Gabriel had his own reality, and he grew stranger by the day.

Eugene felt a stir of pity for the giant with the misformed face, so when Gabriel offered him the pipe, he relented and drew in a lungful. The hashish worked swiftly, cooling him out, and he felt lonesome when Gabriel plunged back into the placid bay where phosphorescent droplets flashed around him like jewel stones tossed after some royal departed.

Then dangling his bare legs over the side of the pirate ship halfway between the resort hotel and the cruise ship freighted with rich Americans, he told himself they were all pirate outlaws, heirs of wicked Port Royale, which sank in the sea in one great upheaval, and they were about to take back what belonged to them from the rich old woman Simon would marry tomorrow.

Then his shoulders slumped. The plan was bizarre, it would never work, and their hopes were fireflies, will-o'-the-wisps, nothing but duppy dreams.

4

Reuben got the actor back to the road. It wasn't easy. The man outweighed him by thirty or forty pounds. Then to St. Vincent's emergency room in twenty minutes flat, don't ask him how. For one thing, he'd left the rig, the compound's communal station wagon, parked on the shoulder of the road. He was driving the actor's Porsche.

They caused a stir. Nurses, X-ray techs, the men swabbing the floors, even blue-haired volunteers craned for a glimpse of Tony Quayle.

Reuben hung in at the emergency room long enough to hear the star explain to the doctor that he'd been felled by a sprained ankle. A surprise, but his not to wonder why. As he fought his way back through the crowd of voyeurs, the man on the examination table called out, "Hold on, my dear fellow! Wait up! What's your name?"

But Reuben ran on down the hall to a bank of phones, followed by a newsman who'd chased an ambulance from a five-car smashup and who caught a shot of him on his Minicam phoning Magda to come pick him up. That explained his picture next day on the front page of the *New Mexican* with the headline: "Can You Identify the Good Samaritan?"

He tried to get back to his painting. But his barber,

the butcher at Kaune's down the hill, a neighbor, and, he suspected, Magda herself had identified the good Samaritan. Pestered by newsmen, he painted with his blinds drawn, gave up his daily runs, and unplugged his phone. When days later he plugged it back in, it rang almost instantly.

"Well, finally, my dear fellow!"

The great man himself.

"Delighted to find you, old chap! You certainly pulled a disappearing act."

Clearly it hadn't worked.

"You did me a service. Give me a chance to repay you."

Did he mean some kind of reward, like maybe money? The cost of paints and canvas had gone astronomical, he owed Magda a month's rent, he was painting by day and waiting tables by night at the Santacafe and cadging scraps off plates on their way back to the kitchen. But though he might be a not-quite-starving artist, the idea of a reward put his back up.

However, shortly after the telephone call he drove out to Tesuque and eased the rig around the curves of a gravel circle marked by a low moss-rock wall surrounding blooming *chamiso* and a weeping birch. He recognized the Porsche and saw in the double garage the rear end of a Range Rover. He'd heard some of the movie people had places out here.

It was a large adobe. Anthony Quayle himself opened the door under the inset *portal* and came forward with outstretched hand. "Delighted, my dear fellow. So good of you to come." And limping slightly he clung to Reuben's arm as they went inside.

Reuben restrained the whistle that rose to his lips. Curvy walls. Arches. Plaster the color and texture of polished leather under concealed lighting. High *latilla* ceilings with vigas and corbels. Acres of Saltillo tile. Expanses of glass framing the mountains. *Santos* in niches. Indian shields that belonged in museums. A flashy Fritz Scholder over the bar. The living room was as big as a lobby, with what was known in local hotels as a conversational grouping in front of a walk-in fireplace. In the presence of such wealth Reuben turned instant snob.

With a deprecating smile, Quayle indicated his ankle and waved in the general direction of the bar. "Would you mind, old chap?"

Reuben poured a Chivas on the rocks for Quayle, and a Chivas with soda for himself, then sat on the edge of the couch holding his drink in both hands. They faced each other across an expanse of black slate coffee table, chatting about the views and the weather and the prospects for snow on the mountain. He inquired about the ankle.

Anthony Quayle smiled, and the charm suddenly radiating off the man both drew Reuben and made him uncomfortable. "It flares up if I'm on it too much. It's been weak from childhood. A lorry backfired, you see, and my pony reared up and reeled over and came down on my foot."

Right, the man was a Brit. Soon out of small talk, Reuben turned to the painting over the fireplace. It looked like a Jackson Pollock. Waste of paint, he thought, for he was young and arrogant. How soon could he get out of here?

When he surfaced he heard, ". . . very grateful . . . don't know what I . . . when you happened to come along . . . may have saved my life."

Right. Dead of a sprained ankle.

"You see," Quayle said, "for the first time in my life I'm venturing into production." When Reuben didn't respond he hurried on. "I mean I'm producing my first film. It's set in the West Indies. We're due to start shooting very soon, and it's disastrous to alarm the backers with health problems. Anyway, I'm offering you the job, and I do hope you'll take it."

Reuben was suddenly alert.

"I need somebody I can trust to take care of the place. I'm so seldom here. And of course there's a stipend."

There had to be a catch. "You mean, like, live out here? You don't even know me."

Tony Quayle chuckled and said, "You're twenty-six years old. Your father is dead. Your mother lives in Brooklyn. And you spent the summer somewhere near here as artist on an archaeological dig."

Reuben wasn't crazy about the idea of being investigated. He crossed one leg over his other knee, picked at the loose sole of his worn-out running shoe, and said he didn't own a car.

"Oh, well, if you don't mind ferrying me back and forth from the airport now and then, you can use the Porsche. It just sits in airport parking when I'm on the Coast."

Apartment. Stipend. Porsche.

"You'd be doing me a favor, old chap. The house is isolated. It's not easy to find someone you can trust. Of course there's the housekeeper, but she's only here during the day."

Still Reuben hesitated, distracted by the film of perspiration on Anthony Quayle's upper lip.

"Of course when I'm here," the actor said, "we'd both have our privacy. Though I want you to feel right at home, no need to make yourself scarce." Then that disarming smile. "You might want to look at the apartment. It's right down that passage."

He thinks he's got me, Reuben thought.

Cautious and skeptical, he investigated a bright apartment attached to one wing of the house and looking out on the mountains in the distance. It opened onto a courtyard with a swimming pool. He allowed himself a breathy whistle. The place had a spotless kitchen-dining area, a large bedroom-bath-dressing-room suite, and a sizeable living room with a big north skylight. Compared to his pad at Magda's compound, it was a palace.

It suited him not only for painting but for escaping daily contact with Tina, who, until last summer, had been his best friend. Then on the archaeological dig where they'd worked all summer as artists, he'd looked at her one day and realized that, unknown to him, his heart had been going about its own affairs. As such feelings can ruin a perfect friendship, and supply if unacted upon an excess of energy in all of one's parts, he'd taken to daily lap swims at Fort Marcy, and workouts with weights, and running along back country trails. It hadn't worked. So maybe moving away from the compound where he had to see her every day would take the edge off and give him time to think.

He asked himself: What are you waiting for? The truth was, he couldn't believe his luck.

Shortly thereafter he drove Tony Quayle to the runway for private planes at the Albuquerque airport, where he was being picked up to fly to the Coast. Then back to Santa Fe in fifty-five minutes flat to pile into the Porsche 911 his clothes, his paints, and sticking out of the backseat of the cabriolet like a Penitente cross, the big old wooden easel he'd bought at a yard sale. He kissed Magda good-bye and looked forward to a time of solitude and work, interrupted at infrequent intervals by brief visits from his famous *patrón*.

That was his plan.

5

He stacked the furniture against the wall and covered the flagstones with drop cloths and rolled out the canvas, his last piece of good linen, not a good shape but expensive—he planned to use every inch. He had the painting in his mind's eye. It was from his summer on the Pajarito Plateau, space retreating in distance, Española Valley to Truchas peaks, little trout mouths leaping at the sky. He thought he could do it. He had a notebook of sketches but he wouldn't look at them. They were just for setting the thing so he could hold onto it in his head. It would evolve, it always did. What he held in the back of his eye was merely a starting place.

He got his stretchers from the only guy in town knew how to get hold of straight wood, and came home with it sticking up in the back of the Porsche. He banged it together out on the patio and brought it in the big room and stretched the canvas on the floor, getting it tight as he could, the gesso would tighten it further. He set it up on two of his four barstools, his old easel propped in the corner, face to the wall, because this was *too big*.

The housekeeper came and went silently—he'd see her big old Mercury Marquis out front, in mint shape, white, with a slightly dented back fender. And sometimes hear the vacuum cleaner going. But he hardly ever glimpsed the woman. Tall, Spanish, Mrs. Pacheco. She kept the big house perfect, ready and waiting for Quayle to appear. But his own place in back toward the mountains was every day more his own—bed unmade, socks on the floor. There was a dishwasher but he never figured out how to use it. He stacked his dishes in the sink. Every day or so he'd run in hot water, squirt in some Joy, and let them soak.

He'd got a good start on the foreground, the sandstone promontory hanging out over the drop, when the first call came, and—humbly, apologetically—his benefactor asked if he'd mind picking up somebody at the airport.

He didn't mind. One thing he knew about himself, say he was into a really good book—Conrad, or Turgenev, and he'd come to a really good part—he'd put down the book and go get himself a bowl of cereal, or make himself a sandwich, then come back to the book, holding onto the low-grade excitement. The Albuquerque run was a little like that break he gave himself when he was excited about what he'd be coming back to. So it was all right, really, the interruption.

He put the top down and started out. It was a fine fall day. Plunging down through the red clay cut of La Bajada, cruising up past semis on the long hills, slowed by orange barrels along the Bernalillo exit—they were always patching the highway—then weaving in and out of fast, tight traffic around Montaño, he made it again in fifty-five minutes.

She was waiting at the curb outside the luggage carousels. He recognized her instantly in spite of the trench coat with the collar up, and wraparound sunglasses, and a scarlet bandana hiding her dusky curls.

"*Quel* relief," she said with that nearsighted frown while he struggled with tapestry luggage in graduating sizes suggesting more than a weekend stay.

As they sped down the hill toward Gibson and the highway north, she removed the shades, pulled off the bandana, and shook out her curly hair.

He'd seen every picture she'd made, not that there were many. A sidelong glance confirmed what he'd suspected: pale amber eyes set in dark lashes, dark skin, and white teeth ever so slightly buck, her looks were exotic enough to obscure her genuine gifts. He envied Quayle. In spite of the age difference, he assumed they were lovers.

She settled deeper into the bucket seat and frankly inspected him. "What did you say your name was?"

Once he got her settled in, it was back to the canvas. He was into the valley. On impulse he moved the river— a river only to him, but a definite woolly line of green back where the landscape started moving *up*. And without a thought he'd given himself a problem. It'd break the whole damn thing in two. But the colors were coming— blue and stone and in the deep recesses, dark, the simplest mix of green and red. Flat, he told himself, no mounting pigment on pigment for now, keep it clean.

The second call came one night later. By then he was glad to hear from Tony Quayle. Zoe McNaire's soft rap- rap had wakened him in the night. "Are you asleep? I could do with some company."

He'd jumped out of bed naked and pulled on a robe and glanced at himself in the mirror and run his hand over his flat little beard.

She was no longer outside his door. He stopped short in the arch to the living room. She was standing at the fireplace with a towel knotted below her waist. Her small perfect navel and her small perfect breasts stared at him across the room.

"In case you thought I was a female impersonator," she said, eyes on his face.

Why would he think that?

"Because," she answered, though he hadn't asked, "I'm broad in the shoulders and small in the hips. It's why I was in such demand as a model."

She moved to one of the couches and sank down with her arms along the back. She was small and sleek and as sensuous as a cat, and her skin was the color of honey. "Those gay clothes designers prefer women to look like boys."

He'd forgotten that chapter in her short history.

"And they liked my ambivalent racial makeup."

The hair and the tawny skin.

"I just wanted you to know I'm the real McCoy."

He'd never doubted it.

She smiled. "Because I've had the operation."

That took its time sinking in. She was a *he*?

She tipped back her head and laughed at him. "I hope you're not buying all this. I do it all the time." Her eyelids and her voice dropped guiltily. "I can't help it. My shrink says it's pathological."

Now she was a liar.

"I'm not a liar," she said playfully. "I'm just weird." A soft little laugh and a shrug. "Some people get off on weird.

"Say something," she teased. "Do you want me?"

Buying time, he went to the bar and dug out tequila and the margarita mix.

She drained her glass like a trooper. "That did it," she

said, stretching and yawning and standing up. "I think I can sleep now."

It was some time before he did.

Back in her room, Zoe McNaire overturned her purse on the bed and raked through the contents. No more cigarettes. Her mouth tasted like an old suede glove anyway. But she had to have something.

In her billfold she found an old roach flattened under cloudy plastic on top of a photograph of her mother. She took out the roach but forgot about it looking at her mother's face, flatter, broader, much darker than her own, and the eyes—wide, sunken—looked back at her. What was it she had always wanted from the woman? Whatever it was, she never got it.

She rolled up on her knees and held the photograph closer to the light. She rubbed a finger over the plastic, but neither it nor her mother's expression got any clearer. She dropped the billfold and dragged her fingers through the rumpled sheets, looking for the roach. Then she stripped off the top sheet and shook it over the carpet. Nothing. She ran her hands frenziedly over the bed, then fell over weeping. She cried with her mouth open till mucous strung down her lip and she couldn't breathe.

Then she had to laugh at herself. After all, she had plenty of money, everybody loved her, she was in the movies.

She hit the remote and the TV came on and the sound lulled her to sleep with the light on.

At dawn Reuben's phone rang again. Mistaking it for the alarm, he fumbled for the clock on the floor where he put it at night because luminous dials bothered him. He liked to sleep in the dark.

The phone rang again. He snatched at it, knocked it to the floor, and, groping, retrieved it. The by-now-familiar voice said, "I hate to be such a bother, old man, but would you mind very much . . . ?"

He sighed and backed out the door looking at his painting.

He was back at the airport by ten. This time there was no disguise. The radical change in the man himself was enough. Maybe only late-night devotees of old movies would recognize Branwell Kane for the slender great actor he had been.

The passenger slept snoring past Bernalillo, then woke to cast hooded glances upon the landscape of sage and buttes and mountains, and launch a monologue that lasted until the Sangre de Cristos loomed ahead. "Devil of a country. Whadda they see in it? Dries out your nose. How do you know where you're going, everything looks alike?" Blah . . . blah . . . blah . . . Followed by off-color jokes guaranteed to repel the least fastidious, at which he laughed till his bulk succumbed to a coughing fit that shook the car.

As they took the off-ramp at St. Francis, Kane sat up and shook himself like a hippo exiting a mudhole. He cleared his throat, pressed the button to lower his window, and spat into the wind.

"What's your name again, son?" he asked.

"Well-well. Do I detect the accents of New York?

"But caretaking can't occupy all your time. So tell me, what do you do all day? I myself have trouble filling time, and there's a great deal of that if you're an actor.

"Well-well, a painter! Houses or pictures?

"So, an artist. What, portraits? Abstractions? Expressionist navelscapes? Ha ha. How about a showing to liven up this—er—conference?"

What kind of conference? Reuben wondered.

Kane coughed and rolled down the window and spat again. Reuben thought this time the backseat was probably the beneficiary. And this from the man who'd played Shakespeare's tragic heroes—Macbeth, Hamlet, Lear. Now he was Falstaff.

Then the actor said in a voice full of breath that suddenly sounded true, "I envy you, young man. I've no pride in my own occupation. What is it? Pretense. Celluloid heroes parroting somebody else's words. A case of multiple personalities masquerading as the performing arts."

Reuben slowed the Porsche as the traffic thickened.

"True, I've a talent for mimicry. I've used it as best I could. I've lent my name to causes deserving of our attention. It's the only way I can justify a life ill spent. Tony's new project interests me, the social-political overtones. God knows I don't go in for period stuff. Deliver me from wigs and codpieces. But I've been reading the history of the Caribbean. I never realized Spain and France and England were far more involved in their interests there than in the mainland of North America. The weather was fine, the soil volcanic and rich, the Indians ripe for slavery. And before many years went by, a wealthy Englishman was said to be 'as rich as a West Indies planter.' "

They left the traffic behind, climbed the hill, and sped down past the opera, slowing finally for the Tesuque exit.

"We here were only a sideshow," Kane said. "The main event took place among the islands."

So, they were coming to Santa Fe in connection with a historical film set somewhere in the Caribbean with social-political overtones relevant to U.S. history. Interesting.

"Did you know that fifty years after the landing of Cristóbal Colón—the Portuguese adventurer we call Columbus, actually I think he was born in Italy—the indigenous Indian population had been wiped out?"

Reuben slowed for the intersection at the Tesuque Market.

"They couldn't survive slavery. They died like those proverbial flies. Some were outright suicides, some willed themselves dead—" a deep sigh wheezed up from the actor's depths "—like Queequeg, Melville's noble harpooner."

The whole car shifted as Reuben felt Kane turn and look at him. "Did you see me as Melville's beautiful sailor?" he asked, and laughed hoarsely with self-contempt. "Do you think I've changed?"

Then abruptly back to the lecture. "After they killed off the Indians, they introduced blacks to the islands. Imagine horrendous ocean voyages lasting months, shackled together in the stinking holds of sailing ships. Cargo, that's all they were. On one voyage, the captain dumped the whole lot overboard to lighten ship and ride out a storm at sea.

"God, men are swine. The blacks who reached port alive must have been magnificent physical specimens. Probably explains all our fantastic black athletes. It's in the genes."

Reuben turned toward the hills and finally nosed down the circle drive. While he retrieved luggage, Kane got out, stretched, yawned, and tried pulling his belt up over his gut. "Well-well, so here we are." He surveyed the hills, the arroyo, the mountains, sky.

"Easy to see why a young painter would settle here." He smiled at Reuben, an engaging smile, and dropped a heavy paw on his shoulder. It was as if on the drive up he'd rehearsed a variety of roles and only now played himself.

That night—or early next morning—another knock at his door. "Are you awake?"

He sat up on the side of the bed and struggled half-asleep into his robe.

She opened the door and let herself in. "I can't sleep," she said, crossing the drop cloths in her bare feet, glancing at the canvas.

She looked at him accusingly. "Did you know the pig was going to be here?"

Kane was the only other person in the house.

She shivered. "Just ignore me," she said. "Go on with what you were doing."

He would have liked to.

"You know why he's doing this, don't you?"

Why who was doing what?

"They're arch rivals, those two." She dropped heavily for such a light body into one of his pigskin chairs.

"Oh, I don't mean they hate each other, nothing like that. Actually," she laughed sardonically, "they *adore* each other. They've each found their ideal nemesis."

She rummaged in the pocket of her robe and came up with a wrinkled cigarette she tried to straighten.

"Men," she said, waving the cigarette between her fingers. Her eyes wandered, registering, he thought, nothing they passed over, certainly not his painting, though it dominated the room.

"The two great actors of our time," she sang, "one a Yank, one a Brit. They've played a lot of the same roles, you know."

He knew. He'd made some comparisons.

"Heroes, villains, Chekov, Shakespeare. I'll bet," she said angrily, "they sit up late in their private projection rooms comparing themselves." The hand with the unlit cigarette waved dismissively. She laughed. "But in this film Kane's character gets dismembered by slaves with cane knives. Kane knives! How fitting!

"Let's change the subject." She turned abruptly and looked at him. "Tell me what you think of me." She said it like a tease, but her eyes were questing, hopeful. She had it all, he thought; how could she be needy?

"You don't find me attractive?"

"You're very attractive."

"That's not what I asked," she said sharply, then eyed him with a sly little smile. "Reuben. I like that name. There's something nice and boyish about you. Me," she teased, flicking an ash from the unlit cigarette—"I'm always involved with rich older men."

Then her face fell into sudden disarray and, alarmed, he thought she was going to cry. "I've lived such a stupid life."

"Come on," he muttered, "you're an actress, you're a star."

"What does that mean? If they have nothing better to do they plunk down a few dollars plus change to see my face big and close up?" She sighed forlornly. "I wish I lived on a Greek island without electricity."

He smiled. "You got something against electricity?"

"Or else in a foreign country and learned to speak the

language like a native. Or done some good in an African village, like Audrey Hepburn.

"How do you want to spend *your* life, *Reuben*?" The emphasis on his name was a kind of dare. "If you don't watch out," she said, "it just slips through your fingers."

Come on, how old could she be? Nineteen? Twenty?

Then another quick change. She got up and crossed the room and trailed languid fingers along his cheek. "Ah, Reuben-Reuben."

He grabbed her wrist. "What's going on, Zoe?"

The exotic face lost its composure. Her eyes widened with fright. Her chin trembled. "Let me go!" she cried.

Startled, he let her go.

"I'm sorry," she whispered, rubbing her wrist though he was sure he couldn't have hurt her. "It's just—I needed company because I woke up terrified."

6

The third guest arrived on his own in a little soft-top 1950s Mercedes. He unwound his lengthy body and put out a hand.

"Nat Reybuhr," he said. "You must be the young man I'm told saved Tony's life."

"It wasn't his heart," Reuben said, "just some kind of spasm." Spasm of the esophagus, Quayle had said. Due to stress.

"Is that what he told you?" Reybuhr retrieved a soft-sided bag from the small backseat. "I'm the script man," he said.

"The writer?"

"Don't I wish. No, it's an adaptation. I'm just a greatly gifted hack."

Were all these famous rich folk filled with self-pity? They reminded him of the houses of the wealthy down in Mexico, disguised with run-down facades. He smiled.

He was wondering what he was supposed to do with these people when the kitchen door opened off the side *portal* and the housekeeper came in, removed her coat, and hung it on a peg. He was greatly relieved to see her.

Early the next morning Anthony Quayle arrived in a limo with tinted windows and a driver. Along with him came a Spaniard with a trim little goatee in an ancient fedora who, when the rear door opened, looked like a man of normal height, but when he stepped down onto the gravel drive, turned out to be about the size of Toulouse-Lautrec. Señor Ribera moved slowly on his stunted legs with the help of a shortened ivory-headed cane. His eyes passed blindly over Reuben to appraise the house.

Next, the limo divulged a tall, distinguished-looking very black man with a cap of iron gray hair, wearing little silver-rim spectacles, who acknowledged introductions in a tenor voice and with an air of amusement. "Armisted Whatley," he said, "of the Jamaica Historical Society." He shook hands around and nodded to Reuben there at the top of the steps.

After Whatley the novelist Datrey Moss, a slight, coffee-colored young man chatting in a soft voice over his shoulder with the director.

The director was a woman.

"Are we all assembled?" the Jamaica historian sang out in his high, lilting voice with the British accent of the islands. The idea seemed to amuse him.

While Reuben wondered who would handle the rapidly accumulating pile of luggage, the Jamaican novelist asked in a voice so soft and grave it seemed to rebuke the historian's gaity, "Has Dame Charlotte arrived?"

"She's in Santa Fe," Tony Quayle said. "She's staying with someone named Waldheimer out on the Old Santa Fe Trail."

Reuben was relieved to hear it. Like the host of a country inn, he'd begun to think he'd overbooked.

Tony Quayle, famous forehead ridged with sincere apologies, was looking at him. "My dear fellow, I'm sure you know the Old Santa Fe Trail much better than I do. I wonder if you would very much mind . . . ?"

Reuben had begun to look his gift horse in the teeth.

7

He avoided the highway and took the narrow winding road to town. He wanted time to think. His painting had lapsed, his solitude evaporated, and, damn it, he was being used.

Who do they think they are?

Scratch that. Everybody knows who they are.

All right, what made them think they could use him as an errand boy?

Apartment, stipend, Porsche, swimming pool—you sold yourself, answered the voice of conscience.

He squirmed. Come on, they're small favors.

For a mile or two he tried to enjoy the Porsche. A silver BMW closed the distance behind him, waited for a straight stretch, and saluted as it passed. He answered with a half gesture of his own, but he knew the salute was for the Porsche.

The whole thing was a downer. Tony Quayle was using him as a lackey. That was the story in Hollywood, wasn't it? Everybody sucking up to whoever stood on the next rung up the ladder? The man must be used to it. As for himself, he wanted nothing.

But the voice of conscience chided: apartment, Porsche, stipend, pool?

Come on, he argued, in return for all that, what're a few trips in the sports car?

But no, that wasn't it. What it was—he sat deeper in the bucket seat—he was feeling lousy about himself. He had always taken his self-respect for granted, not suspecting that it could fluctuate wildly depending on . . . He settled for "circumstances."

The powerful motor purred out of the canyon and up the hill past Bishop's Lodge. A noisy step-side pickup roared by, descending with little explosions and black puffs of smoke. Two sets of admiring eyes under the bills of baseball caps turned to look at him. The Porsche again. He realized till now he'd been enjoying that, and the knowledge made him squirm.

Suddenly he envied those two fellows their pickup, their baseball caps, their easy camaraderie.

Come on, you're feeling sorry for yourself.

With that revelation came a wave of self-contempt. Could it be he envied Tony Quayle and his friends their wealth, their ease, their expensive toys?

Face it, he told himself, they make you feel small.

He jabbed the button and the radio came on. A woman advised him about stocks. Her husband quibbled a little but essentially backed her up. They chuckled companionably. He *hated* that—news anchors, talk-show people, pretending they really liked each other when you knew it was an act for the listening audience, all of it fake. It really bothered him. Everything bothered him. Why did everything bother him?

He hit the button again and silenced the happy pair.

Money, he mouthed. Nations, institutions, families rise or fall to the tune of it. Language and customs and gods may differ, but the faith in money was sound the world over.

What would happen, he wondered, if that faith failed? He smiled. CEOs would jump from tall buildings.

He sped down the hill to the north leg of the Paseo and stopped for the light.

The trouble with capitalism: the big fish eat the little fish. The trouble with communism: takes half the population as bureaucrats to control what the other half gets in the way of an extra room and bath.

He gave up on global economics.

He crossed Alameda and gunned up the diagonal corner of Canyon Road, swerved right onto Garcia, and ran up the hill toward his home compound, where he slowed. He badly wanted to turn in but made himself drive past. At the top of the hill he took a left at the Y that put him on the Old Santa Fe Trail.

Once off the pavement, he slowed to protect the Porsche's paint job from the gravel. He tried reading names on mailboxes, thought he was too far out, was about to backtrack when he caught a glimpse of the name. He braked and backed, and squinted into the morning light.

Waldheimer.

He shifted to low and wound up a twisting gravel drive past corrals and horseless stables and some kind of hutches and finally emerged from the piñon and junipers into a clearing.

The old Southwest-style mansion—Christ, it was real adobe—rose in levels against the foothills, its expanses of glass black now with the morning sun behind the house. He never wore a watch. According to the Porsche's clock it was still shy of ten A.M.

When he cut off the motor he could hear the piñon jays foraging noisily under the evergreens.

8

Zoe McNaire sat up on the edge of the pool and grabbed her towel.

Branwell Kane chuckled emerging from the house. "Too late for modesty. I'm well acquainted with your charms, Zoe." With a sigh like a pneumatic cushion, he let himself down on one of the lounges.

"What are you doing here, pig?"

"You know very well, Zoe, I've a certain sympathy with a film of this kind."

"I'd never have signed on if I'd known you had anything to do with it."

"Oh, come, girl. In spite of all I've done for you, you've rocketed your star into a downward spiral. If Marilyn couldn't get away with theatrics that sent production costs soaring, surely you can't. No, I'd say you're lucky Tony can see only you as Esme."

She'd been lying on her stomach sunning herself when he appeared in an enormous pair of shorts, the bound script in hand, and eased himself down, dropping sandals off feet surprisingly small for the rest of him. His chest with its grizzled hair and pendulous breasts heaved from the exertion.

"It's true the part fits your unique endowments," he said. It pleased him that he knew how to get to her.

As always, her rage welled up in the form of tears. Though she hated it, she couldn't seem to help herself. Her shrink said it was pain she was feeling, that she interpreted it as rage because she found anger a more acceptable emotion.

"You know I can act," she said. "Why can't you admit it?" One day she'd get a part because of her talent, not because of her goddam looks.

"Tsk tsk, come now, little one, if your mestiza face is a box-office draw, it's no different from the bleached big-tit blondes of yesteryear filling a particular demand."

"You goddam pedophile. The older you get, the younger your victims." In spite of herself, her voice broke. "I was a child!"

"Oh, come. You weren't the first and you won't be the last to throw your delicious body at me with an eye to your career."

"I loved you! You're fat and mean and old and ugly, but I loved you!"

"Did you really?"

Was he calling her a liar, or did he really want to know? There was a certain wistfulness in his voice. Sometimes underneath the mockery he was serious, but she could never tell when.

"You know I did." She bit her lip and controlled a new upsurge of grief. "I wanted to live with you, look after you in your—"

"Don't try to make me feel old!" His sigh rumbled on his lips. "We've had this exchange before, girl. It bores me."

"I hate you, Kane," she whispered. Then she wished she could call that back. She'd always called him Kane. It had been her term of endearment. "You made me do something abominable and I'll never forgive you."

"Come now, you know better than to upset yourself. You're well aware of what can happen."

"I wanted to keep it! I didn't care if you never saw it, never acknowledged it or did anything for it, it was mine and *I wanted it*! But your reputation had to come first!"

He laughed. "What reputation?"

"You've sired so many brats one more wouldn't have mattered. Oh, I know you thought they'd get you for statutory rape, but I would have denied to my death you were the—"

"Ah, but your dear mama was threatening me with this DNA thing. And as you know, Mama likes money."

"Just shut up about Mama!"

She rose and stepped to the edge of the pool and dived, splashing Kane, sandals, script, and all.

He chuckled and ducked and narrowed his eyes against the New Mexico sun, watching her cut like a bright tropical fish through the water. His hands fluttered, moving of their own volition to sketch the remembered shape of her small firm buttocks lifting toward him. She had on a bright blue Skidoo bathing suit. She was small and slight, with skin the color of sun through a snifter of brandy.

She was right, he thought grimly. If they got any younger he would be eating pullets straight from the egg.

Branwell Kane held the human race in contempt, not least of all himself. And particularly women because they let themselves be drawn to vermin like him. Conversely, he viewed their beauty as Venus's-flytraps. Sometimes this contempt had shown on-screen, lending the sensual scenes of his young manhood a touch of deadly violence he thought fitting for the disgusting act he pursued with such diligence.

But in this film, thank God, he was no romantic hero.

He'd consented to the role partly because of his commitment to minority causes, the one thing he thought gave his life meaning. But even so, he suspected his motives were selfish, for in his secret soul he identified with the disenfranchised. For all his fame and wealth, he knew he was one of them.

He watched Zoe thoughtfully as she spread her arms for a surface dive and disappeared in a swirl of water. She reappeared, reached for the curb of the pool, and pulled herself up, glancing to see that he watched. He smiled and raised his glass. Caught looking, she let go and sank to the bottom, and he knew she would not look at him again. And with all his wealth and nuisance fame and silly fans across the known world, he felt bereft and fat and ugly as a walrus.

He slid in the chaise till his toes disappeared and he looked with disgust down the ridges and rolls of his ample girth. Soon he would stroll into a scene like Sidney Greenstreet, majestic in white, gravity claiming his jowls but stomach strutting before him, announcing his entrance. The scene could be *Casablanca* or *The Maltese Falcon*.

Señor Ribera was surprised to find it had been left to him to unpack his own suitcase. In Spain at an illustrious house that would have been done for him. As he stretched on his toes to hang up his suits, he reflected that there seemed to be no servants. Weren't all American filmmakers rich?

He had been offered a generous sum to act as consultant, and generous sums were convincing to Señor Ribera. Also this western part of the country had once been New Spain, settled by his compatriots. His ancestor, the valorous Pedro Cárdenas, had returned to Castile after making his fortune in the conquest of Peru, thereby assuring his welcome at the Spanish court and gaining a knighthood that Señor Ribera dreamed one day of reclaiming.

He opened an easily accessible lower drawer and laid in his shirts. Carefully. If slightly frayed they were still very fine, as were his undergarments. And nothing would soon be replaced. His ancestor's gold had long since gone to the glory of Spain in foreign wars, and Señor Ribera made his way in society by his arrogance, his wardrobe, and the assurance with which he dispensed misinformation, though at times, in his dark nights of the soul, he suspected it was only that they preferred their court jesters to be dwarfs, or nearly. Perhaps it made them feel larger. Well, he despised his benefactors, if anything more than he suspected they despised him.

Señor Ribera sighed and climbed with some difficulty onto the bed. No fruit in the room to tide him over until luncheon. No flowers, either. This lapse filled him with contempt. For the house of a rich man—and of such houses he was a connoisseur—this one left much to be desired.

And on top of everything, the presence of *the Moors*.

He briefly considered the two Jamaicans. Then sighing he wondered when luncheon would be served. He hoped it would be edible.

Armisted Whatley of the Jamaica Historical Society knocked and, without waiting to be acknowledged, peered around the door. "Are you all right, my boy?" he asked anxiously.

"You knew she would be here," Datrey Moss said gently.

The historian sighed and quietly closed the door. "I suppose I did."

The novelist laid aside his notebook and his reading glasses. "Why didn't you warn me, Army?"

Whatley turned back to the younger man. "This is your chance, Datrey. It wouldn't do for you to avoid it."

"I'd prepared myself to meet her in Jamaica."

The historian patted the young man's arm.

"She's uncommonly lovely, don't you think?"

"She is indeed," Armisted Whatley said.

"Do you think she . . . ?"

"Of course not. It was a long time ago."

The historian crossed to the window and addressed the mountains through the glass. "What can they be thinking, hiring that idiot, that know-nothing?"

Datrey Moss tossed his notebook aside. He had been jotting notes for his newest project, a novel set in the modern Carribean contrasting the poverty of the inhabitants with the wealth of the tourists.

Datrey Moss wanted desperately to capture, in a literature that would last, the warmth of a people and the richness of a culture. But with Jamaica's history and poverty, and what he considered its unsatisfactory politics, to do so might render his people merely picturesque and himself a dilettante. On the other hand, he feared that focusing so single-mindedly upon the country's problems might make him nothing more than a political propagandist.

Whatley said, "I have met this fool time after time at lectures, dispensing his version of Caribbean history. His ignorance is appalling."

The young novelist looked upon the older man with his iron gray skullcap, his tall strong body, and his ebony complexion as both physically and psychically a pure being, his blood apparently never diluted by that of another race.

"Don't let the fool disturb you, Army," the young man murmured, his mind on other things.

Whatley jiggled the change in his pocket and said in his high-pitched, breaking voice, "Why can I not suffer fools lightly?"

Datrey Moss smiled. "According to a high authority, it's one of the 'fardels' we must bear—'the pangs of despised love, the proud man's contumely . . . the spurns that patient merit of the unworthy takes . . .' "

Whatley chuckled. "How could Shakespeare possibly have known that last?" He turned from the window. "I'm afraid I have very little 'patient merit,' " he said. He clapped the young novelist gratefully on the shoulder. "You keep me sane, friend. You are a fugitive from the law of averages." He'd forgotten who said that.

He changed the subject. "Devil take this old woman!"

"Perhaps she'll be amenable and accept the offer. It strikes me as generous."

"If she holds out for her price much longer I'm afraid they'll look at other locations. Jamaica's economy could be out millions."

"Maybe the new husband has talked some sense into her. He's got to be into wealth. What other reason would he have for marrying her?"

In the next room, Margarite Barbon was pacing, trying to recover from her earlier encounter with Tony Quayle.

"You said you'd try Palance again, Tony. You promised!"

"I did," he countered.

"Did what? Tried? Or promised!"

He chuckled. The man was maddening. "His agent

says he's out of the country, and he's committed for some time to other projects."

"I don't believe you! You let me think you had him sewed up. And now you've signed Kane."

She should never have let him talk her into doing this picture. On the drive up, the accents in the limousine had unnerved her, recalling as they did the islands. They would be on location in Jamaica for most of the filming. She paced, her mouth moving as she reproved herself.

"We could do most of those scenes in the studio," she'd argued.

Quayle's eyebrows went up. "But Margarite, I've been under the impression you always prefer shooting on location."

He was right. How could she argue?

She pulled the cord and opened the drapes and absently registered Branwell Kane on the wrought-iron chaise. Annoyed at the sight, she turned back to the room and paced again, hugging herself. She hadn't any objections to months away from Illusionland. On the contrary, it might rid her head and heart of the cliques and schemes, the pathetic barrages of name-dropping, and the anxious, empty laughter of people on the make.

Had she ever been like that? Falsified herself? Posed and postured? Certainly she had never slept with any mogul in exchange for favors.

She wondered at her need, ever so often, to reiterate all the insufferable things she had not done. It was like kneeling outside the confessional as a girl and ferreting out the sins she would take to the priest waiting behind the curtains. Only now the confession was to herself.

All right, she had stepped on rivals along the way, she had allowed certain despised people to befriend her because she needed their introductions. Out of her need, almost visceral, to make films, she had neglected some who'd loved her. That had gained her a reputation for coldness, but who had time for distractions?

When she was younger she'd allowed attachments to interfere with her work, once refusing a spot as assistant director on a film shot in Italy because she could not tear herself from the arms of a lover.

That would never happen again. Alone in the room she smiled ironically. Lovers come and go. She would never again let her center stray outside herself. For in love she had often been uncertain, anxious, miserable—all weaknesses she despised. But working she was confident to the point of arrogance, and most important, she was always happy.

In the dresser mirror her features were sharp, and her short red hair so thick her image struck her as top-heavy. She turned away, thinking about Datrey Moss's book. She both loved and hated it. The young novelist seemed to think he had some answers to the island's problems. Where Jamaica was concerned, she no longer even knew the questions.

She wondered what demons might descend once she was back there. All her adult life she had fought off the fear of beastly memories only then to suffer nostalgia for the place's seductive charms—tropical waters, lush foliage, the warm laughter, thin black limbs and faces set off by the vibrant colors of costumes. And the birds. She heard them now.

Outside, Zoe McNaire performed an inexpert dive, splashing Kane there on the lounge. Margarite Barbon raised her eyes to the Sangre de Cristos. No wonder this place had become second home to the stars. Clearly it was beautiful and peaceful. As they'd approached Santa Fe the landscape had reminded her of a frozen sea, stilled by the hand of God. She and the Almighty had once enjoyed a close relationship. She saw her child self in the navy blue jumper, her knees vulnerable above the mandatory white knee socks—the school uniform in St. Ann's Parish.

Her religious upbringing at the convent school seldom intruded now upon her life, but though a nonbeliever in any organized cosmology, she welcomed the infrequent glimpses of some somnolent part of her consciousness that kept straying into the nebulous regions of the divine and the damned.

She threw herself down on the bed and lay for a time staring at the ceiling but found she couldn't relax. She got up, straightened her clothes, pulled a comb through her hair, and told herself, All right, I have to go back sometime. It might as well be now.

She threw a sweater over her shoulders and opened the door to the hall, and collided with a soaking wet, trembling Zoe McNaire.

"Oh! I'm so sorry!" the girl cried, wrapping her towel tighter, and, ducking her head, she circled around the director.

Margarite Barbon hesitated, then reluctantly took her by the shoulders. "What's wrong? Why're you crying?"

Zoe raised an anguished face and swiped the mucous off her upper lip with her finger.

"Come," the director said. Leading her into the bedroom, she shoved Zoe into the shower to let the warm water take away the chill, then fetched her a dry towel.

Zoe sobbed, letting the towel trail to the floor.

"Dry yourself off!" the director commanded. And when the girl only looked at her, "Here, give me." She took the towel and ran it roughly head to foot over Zoe McNaire, who stood limply before her.

"Get out of that wet suit and put this on." She handed Zoe her own robe, and Zoe obediently did as she was told.

Margarite Barbon glanced through the sliding door and saw Branwell Kane still there in the wrought-iron chaise. She turned Zoe away from the sight and shoved her down in a chair.

"Feel better now?"

Zoe nodded. "You're very kind."

The director laughed. "Not kind, efficient."

"I admire you ever so much," Zoe said.

To hide her pleasure, the director turned away. She watched Kane pull himself out of the chaise, stoop to the pool, and splash his sweating self with water.

"He's a very great actor, isn't he," Zoe said wistfully. Tears gone, she looked out on the patio and pulled the robe tight around her. "I know I'm lucky."

"Lucky?"

"For the opportunity to work opposite him."

The director said, heading for the door, "For God's sake dry your hair!"

Startled, Zoe thought: I knew it! The woman can't stand me.

Nat Reybuhr lay on his stomach clutching the South-western counterpane with his eyes clenched shut. A few minutes earlier, unpacking his toilet articles he'd absently pulled a comb through his longish hair, and a hank came out in his hand. It was still in his fist as he lay there on his stomach with his eyes clenched tight.

He tried to get hold of himself. If they succeeded with the greedy old woman, in a few days they'd be leaving

Santa Fe and flying to Miami, the lot of them. Then on to Montego Bay.

Did he dare have the test in Jamaica?

"Anything the matter?" Kane had asked in their moment alone. "You look like hell."

"It's nothing. A virus."

Kane snorted. "That's all we need. I hope the damn thing's not catching."

Not in any contact we're likely to have, Reybuhr thought bitterly. He admired the man, considered him the foremost actor of his time, and he'd looked forward to watching Quayle-the-director turn a Nat Reybuhr script into its own kind of reality. But now . . .

His skin felt slimy. He'd broken into a sweat.

Forty-seven years old, his reputation in the industry assured, twice nominated for Oscars though he'd never got one. But he told himself the nomination was the greater honor, coming as it did from his peers, while the award sometimes honored the elusive ends of Hollywood politics. Was all that to come to nothing? All the expressions of pity and compassion in the world would not convince him they didn't think in their heart of hearts that whoever got the virus had brought it on himself.

Nat Reybuhr liked his work. Despite the frustrations of collaboration, when he sometimes saw his script decimated, he enjoyed all of it. He liked being on the set, hearing his lines and what the actors did with them, sometimes improving on the original but sometimes confusing their meaning with their own lugubrious interpretations.

Lying there on the bed in Quayle's Santa Fe house, he for the moment forgot his plight. God, to have at his disposal only British actors like Tony Quayle. They didn't have to try, with their misinterpretations of Method, to make the character *sympathetic*. They could play fools as fools, clowns as clowns, villains as villains. They *acted*, for God-sake, they didn't have to *become* the character. He wished Quayle were playing the plantation owner instead of Kane.

He thought of the young Jamaican novelist. The man had everything—genius, self-assurance, looks. A delicately carved young god. And he wrote with such a sure voice it was clear he'd never doubted himself. Working from the novel had been both a pleasure and a pain, the pleasure of the pace and the sure, clear dialogue, the pain of knowing none of it was his.

But he'd put his stamp on it. This script was the best he'd ever done. He'd improved on the book, broadened its scope, made it more dramatic, more significant to the present century. This time he might really take home one of the naked little bastards.

He buried his face in the pillow. If he lived long enough.

Anthony Quayle climbed with some difficulty the ridge behind his house. His foot still gave him twinges, and he favored it. The infrequent chest pains were something else. As he climbed he gripped in his pocket the little bottle of nitro he always carried with him.

He found a rock saddle and let himself down to survey his domain. He watched with interest an inaudible exchange between Branwell Kane and Zoe McNaire down by the pool. Then the young actress rose and dived, splashing Kane—he could tell by the way the actor flinched.

Quayle smiled. This house would do, its setting appealed, though he would have preferred the real thing, like the Petaluma adobe, surviving as it had from when California was part of Mexico, originally enclosing its huge central court on all four sides so that the *hidalgo*

patrón could, at the hint of hostilities, close the gates that
were tall and broad enough to admit a six-mule team
pulling a top-heavy freight wagon loaded with furs and
staples, and perhaps firearms, or gold and silver. He had
once, in his early days in Hollywood, spent weeks at the
place, the locale of a John Wayne western he'd played in.
With a place like that, he could barricade the gates, not to
keep out predators, but to imprison his guests.

A figure moved behind one of the windows. Margarite
Borbon. She had not been easy to bring on board. She'd
wanted another actor, not Branwell Kane. She agreed the
man was a consummate professional, but he had been
known to throw away a script and improvise.

"Often improving upon the lines," Quayle had reminded
her. But how, she asked, was she to keep the reins in her
own hands when someone willfully wrested them from her?

"Sometimes, if you let go," he'd said, "you get marvels."

Overlooking what he humorously thought of as "his
spread," he argued about the only actor he had ever
envied: I know the man's a bastard, but a remarkable
bastard, and he brings out the best in the other actors.

He knew because it had happened to him when they'd
once made a film together. Apparently without even
trying, Kane projected an uncanny, controlled intensity
that drew from the other actors whatever they had that
could match it. Tony Quayle admired Kane's genius
almost as much as his ruthlessness.

Nor had Margarite wanted Zoe McNaire, arguing that
her temperament alone could add time and costs to the
production. She was right, though he thought these were
good reasons rather than the real ones. He doubted Barbon
herself knew the real reason, but he thought he did.

Still, he had no choice. He had to have Zoe McNaire.

Branwell Kane had made it clear he would not come on board without her. So he'd humbly agreed with the director but insisted the girl had cleaned up her act, something he was far from sure of.

Though she couldn't very well say it, he knew the director did not want him with her on location, so he'd been sure to mention it was only for a little while to attend to financial minutiae and take them off her hands. But in exchange for getting his way on the other questions, he'd had to bow to many of her demands. She'd gotten the cinematographer and film editor of her choice, and final authority over the script.

Ah well—the famous mouth twisted into a smug little smile—none of that much mattered in regard to his private scenario: he had brought these people together to test a theory. Also, like units of blood for the dying, or a serial killer's lust, his needs accelerated with his failing health: no longer a participant, he satisfied his craving for *Sturm und Drang* through manipulation, pulling the strings and watching people jump and dangle.

The sun was rising on a cloudless day. He lifted the dark aviator glasses nested in his thinning hair and settled them on the bridge of his nose. He'd left acting because of the secret of his health and because he thought he'd lost his looks—not that he'd ever been handsome, but now the face confronting him in the mirror was as gray as an oyster with two eyes swimming in it. Repulsive. But he'd left also because of a growing impatience. A mere actor, even a star, was at the mercy of script, camera, makeup, director, and a thousand small exigencies of schedule. But a producer had power. It was like playing God.

Except—he frowned behind the dark glasses—in this case God was at the mercy of a stubborn old woman.

9

Reuben entered behind old Jack and saw the wolf on the hearth and the two old girls going at it ninety to nothing, one in a wheelchair with an oxygen tube running up her front and branching into her nose, and a mask of makeup liberally and haphazardly applied, lips a bright red squiggle and springy curls that had to be a wig. And under the oxygen tube, a veritable breastplate of gold, with emeralds the size of buckles.

She was laughing, poking holes in the air with her cane. "And the time we bobbed our hair and stole Richard's clothes and put on fake mustaches—"

"*You* put on the fake mustache."

"—and went off to that naughty place in Soho."

"Oh, I don't think it was Soho."

Each had a glass in hand and sipped liberally. He thought they might be the least bit tipsy.

"Oh, yes it was. It was *you,* Perdy, said we must *live!*"

"I distinctly recall the whole scheme was yours, Lottie."

"And no idea it was a gay place."

"We didn't even know the term."

"When that man tried to pick you up you forgot your disguise and if I hadn't grabbed you . . ."

50

They rocked with laughter, glasses all but empty.

"He must have thought I was daft!"

"He was very pretty, as I recall. All those handsome unavailable men!"

"Oh, wasn't it fun! Who was it said youth is wasted on the young?"

"Sounds like Wilde."

"Well, we didn't waste it!"

"I'd like to do it all over again."

They were suddenly sober.

"You're brighter than me, Perdy, you always were," said the one in the wheelchair. Perdy. That would be Perdita Waldheimer. Gray slacks, short salt-and-pepper hair cut in choppy waves. "Tell me what you make of all those lights and tunnels, and greetings from dead persons of one's acquaintance."

"I know no more about it than you do, Lottie."

"Well, I must say I find the prospect unnerving. I *would* like to know what it's all about!"

"So would we all," Perdita Waldheimer said. "Why do you think they're out there probing the heavens with their space vehicles and Hubble telescopes? They're in a veritable *frenzy* to find out what it's all about."

"I must say, Perdita, I'm not enjoying this final stretch of the journey. It's a bloody bad show."

"But my dear, think of the alternative." Perdita sighed.

"Well, I say it's for the birds. Though to think of it, I've never seen an elderly sparrow. I've never seen an elderly bee. I'm particularly fond of my apiary. Fascinating creatures—all slaving away for their queen. Rather like our own royals back home, eh?" She laughed. "Only I don't hold with all that. I'm at heart an egalitarian."

"You, Lottie!"

"Oh come, don't laugh. I didn't start out as a Dame but just a dame, as your Yanks would have it. Just after the invasion, I'll never forget it—"

"I know, Charlotte dear. You were very brave. Must have been perfectly dreadful." It sounded like Perdita had heard that story before.

"Oh, I don't know. It was rainy and mucky, and often our vehicles bogged down, but right down the valley of the Rhine with Ike! I've never lived so vitally since."

Perdita said, "Yes, yes, I'm sure."

When old Jack cleared his throat, she turned cheerfully. "Yes, what is it?" She reeled out her pince-nez and settled them on her nose and peered. "Oh, I see. What is it, young man?"

Reuben introduced himself, and a lanky guy dressed like a fashion plate rose from the wing chair where till then he'd been hidden from view. He put out his hand. "Simon Blakemore."

The bridegroom. They shook hands and Reuben said he'd come to drive the couple out to Tesuque.

"This is Dame Charlotte," Perdita said.

Reuben nodded to the gold-armored front, and Dame Charlotte tapped the young groom on his elegantly clad leg.

"Yes-yes," she said, picking up from the floor what looked like a football with a handle, her oxygen tank. "Come, Simon, let's get this tiresome business over with. We'll see you this evening, Perdita," she sang out, settling the football in her lap. The groom leapt behind her wheelchair.

Reuben looked in vain for the bride, but Perdita rose and took his arm and he had no choice but to make his slow way with her to the terrace, where Dame Charlotte was waving her cane indignantly at the Porsche.

"They can't expect me to ride in that!"

"Of course not, dear," Perdita said. "Jack, go get the Caddy."

The Caddy turned out to be a vintage gold Cadillac in mint condition, which old Jack, sitting high behind the wheel, drove around front. The bridegroom lifted Dame Charlotte like a child and carried her down the flagstone steps and tucked her into the roomy backseat, then folded the wheelchair and stowed it in the trunk.

Perdita Waldheimer smiled and waved and took old Jack's unsteady arm. They turned back to the house.

Standing by the driver-side door, Reuben waited for the bride to appear.

"Well, young man, what are we waiting for?" Dame Charlotte said. And the groom met Reuben's eyes with a touch of defiance and pointedly took the blue-veined hand.

Reuben flushed with sudden knowledge: the pair in the backseat was the bridal couple. He slid quickly under the wheel. After the Porsche, driving the Caddy was like piloting the *Titanic*.

Tony Quayle greeted the couple himself. "Ah, Dame Charlotte, you're here!"

"Obviously," Dame Charlotte said, her voice rising on the last syllable.

"Come in, come in, we're all waiting."

Quayle tried to take a hand with the wheelchair, but Dame Charlotte barred him with her cane. "Simon!"

Then, the football in her lap, Reuben on one side and the groom the other, they climbed with the wheelchair to the terrace and set her down. Simon Blakemore wheeled her toward the door.

Quayle snapped his fingers at Reuben. "Give us a hand, old man."

Reuben's jaw tightened. He held open the door and helped the wheelchair pass, but that did it. He was through.

As Tony Quayle ushered them into the house, he rounded the corner outside and returned to the apartment where he grabbed his clothes still on hangers, emptied drawers, stuffed everything in his duffle and left the pile on the bed. He folded the drop cloths and tested the painting. It was dry. That figured. He removed it from the stretchers, took the stretchers apart, rolled the painting, scooped up his paints, collapsed the old easel, and piled everything outside the door on the patio, and for one last time admired the view of the mountains. Then he headed for the living room to tell Tony Quayle he was leaving.

10

As he approached, the place was so quiet he thought they'd all gone. But they were there, sitting glumly in silence. The tension in the room was palpable. He waited in the doorway trying to catch Quayle's eye.

Datrey Moss said in his soft voice, "But Dame Charlotte, Turtle Bay Plantation has every natural setting the script calls for."

"Did you have my plantation in mind when you wrote your book, young man?"

The novelist looked at the toes of his shoes.

"I found very little truth in your fiction," she said.

"My dear lady," Armisted Whatley said in his strange, high-pitched voice, "as you know, we have been fortunate in attracting American film companies to Jamaica. There was the James Bond and—"

"Lot of good that's done."

"It brings us revenues."

"And corruption."

"But, Dame Charlotte," Anthony Quayle said, "all we ask is three short months."

"In three short months the damage could be irreparable—to plantings, to wildlife, to roads meant only for farm equipment."

55

Tony Quayle said, "We will pay you for any damage we cause."

"Pay!" Dame Charlotte exclaimed. "How can you compensate me for a nutmeg tree that takes years to bear?"

Watching from the archway, Reuben thought Tony Quayle looked worn down but Dame Charlotte looked ready for anything.

Nat Reybuhr stood with his back turned at the window, looking out on the mountains, jingling coins in his pocket and rocking impatiently on his toes. "We can shoot the film in Hawaii. Plenty of tropical scenery there—mountains, waterfalls, streams, ravines. And a state government willing and eager to cooperate."

Armisted Whatley's amused look returned. "And everything twice as expensive as in the Caribbean."

"Where would you get your extras for the slave uprising?" Zoe McNaire asked, and giggled. "You could make it a pineapple plantation and an uprising of coolies."

The novelist looked pained.

Tony Quayle said, "Dame Charlotte, you and I both know Turtle Bay Plantation is unique. Without it, we'll have to move cast and crew by sea and air to no less than three other Caribbean islands to find the locations we need. But time is of the essence. We'll do that if we have to."

The old lady said, "I doubt it." She looked at her bridegroom. "Simon?"

Simon Blakemore said from deep in one of the armchairs, "Let's be honest. The last hurricane cut into the beaches and affected vegetation for twenty-five miles inland on the Mexican coast, and sent the native birds to more hospitable environments. It demolished St. Thomas and damaged your other islands. Your alternate locales are no longer possibilities. And," he added, "we are aware that most of your crew has already arrived and is waiting in Montego Bay."

Margarite Barbon chuckled and stood up, glass in hand—it looked like the remains of a Bloody Mary. She walked to the fireplace and turned to face them. "We all know the film calls for more than waterfalls and ravines."

For the first time he really looked at the director. She was quirkily attractive with her short, curly copper-colored hair and lively eyes in a face full of freckles.

"The script," she said, "calls for the ruinate and the Cockpit Country. Only Jamaica, and only Turtle Bay Plantation, offers easy access to all these plus the coffee plantations in the highlands. Everyone in this room knows that without the plantation the shooting will have to be postponed while we arrange for alternatives, and if that happens, Tony, you stand to lose financing."

Tony Quayle looked at her—angrily, Reuben thought, for tipping his hand—but before Quayle could say anything Branwell Kane stood up chuckling, tugging his trousers free of his crotch, and lumbered over to stand beside the director.

"Face it, Tony. The lady's got you by the yin-yang. She may be demanding a fortune—" he smiled approvingly at Dame Charlotte "—but a delay could cost you the film."

"My time here is limited," Dame Charlotte said sharply. "Let's get on with the tiresome business."

Señor Ribera found the discussion boring. Talk-talk-talk. These Americans had most of the money in the world—why all the palaver? And look at the gold and jewels draping that old woman; that one necklace alone must be worth a king's ransom. How he hated the British.

They'd stolen the whole Caribbean from Spain. Hadn't Their Catholic Majesties financed the voyage of the *Santa Maria* and her sister ships? But God had stripped his country of wealth and his ancestors of titles, and himself of the height of a man. Life was not fair.

The smells from the kitchen were intriguing, but there they were, spreading their papers on the low coffee table, reading aloud what was jibberish to Señor Ribera. Wasn't anybody hungry?

Then suddenly the old lady seemed to lose her edge. She reached out, groping for her bridegroom's hand. "I must lie down," she said. "Just sign the damn thing, Simon, and find me a bed."

Then the housekeeper appeared from the kitchen and announced they would eat soon. The artist in Reuben admired the woman. Hair in a thick braid wound around her head, piercing black eyes that surveyed them all but kept her aura of privacy.

Once she'd disappeared, he crossed the room in quick strides to Anthony Quayle. "Look, Tony, I need to talk to you."

But Quayle squeezed his arm. "Not now, old chap. Look, we've an empty place for lunch. I'd be obliged if you'd join us."

11

Reuben rated lunch a disaster. On the way into the dining room, Zoe McNaire took the director's arm and said placatingly, "I'm so looking forward to working with you," and Margarite Barbon drew away murmuring, "I see you've recovered." Then Zoe sidled up to him and whispered, "Is she a closet racist?" and laughed a little hysterically.

Once seated, the Jamaican novelist asked Branwell Kane, at one end of the table facing Tony Quayle at the other, if he would be playing the part of Hamish Hamilton.

At which Zoe McNaire knocked over her wine and stained the tablecloth, and Bran Kane laughed softly. "That's right. I'll be playing the brute that has the pleasure of raping you, Zoe."

And the starlet picked up salsa on her spoon and slung it at him. He dodged and it hit the wall and slithered slowly floorward.

Kane's laugh broke the shocked silence. The others chuckled nervously as if the incident had been a light-hearted charade.

Reuben lowered his eyes and shoved the food around on his plate.

Señor Ribera said to the novelist, "It's historically accurate, young man, that your villain is British." He looked a very distinguished man of perfectly normal size sitting there. "By the time the film takes place, the British had wrested the islands by violence and chicanery from my Spanish forebears, who, after all, had brought Christianity to the natives." He lifted a spoonful of soup to his pink lips nested in a clipped beard wrapping his face like a bandage, and daintily blew on it.

Reuben felt Armisted Whatley stiffen beside him. The Jamaica historian said in a voice taut with anger, "Your forebears from Columbus on made slaves of the 'Indians,' as they called them. The fools thought they'd landed in the Indies."

Zoe muttered, "Skip first grade, you might miss that."

Señor Ribera murmured, "Doubtless there were excesses."

"I've expanded the story a bit," Nat Reybuhr said to Datrey Moss—patronizingly, Reuben thought. "I've extended the violence to Cuba and some of the other islands. It's historically accurate."

The young Jamaican paused briefly, then went on dissecting a chicken breast. "With the director's concurrence, I am deleting those additions. The film, like the novel, must focus on Jamaica."

Nat Reybuhr put down his cutlery and looked at Anthony Quayle. "Is this true, Tony?"

Their host went on eating. "Ask the director, Nat. She has final say over the script."

Nat Reybuhr looked at Margarite Barbon. "Without those scenes the film becomes parochial and loses all contemporary relevance."

"And with them," the novelist said softly with his eyes

on his plate, "it becomes nothing more than an outdated swashbuckling romance."

Armisted Whatley said, "The film is about the evils of empire. Anybody's empire."

Zoe McNaire said angrily, "It's about the horrors of racism—one race wiped out, another imported as slaves!"

"It's about greed and rapacity."

"Whose, Tony? Yours?" Branwell Kane said, chuckling. "Come on, man! You're making this film because you know we're all basically cannibals. We love violence and an enemy we can hate, preferably of a different color. Barring that, religion will do."

Tony Quayle said, "And you're in it, Branwell, because you think it'll make us take a good look at ourselves, ask ourselves how much suffering we're willing to tolerate on this globe." He laughed coldly. "Maybe it'll provide a few animated conversations over a good steak, but you're a fool if you think it'll change anything. For all your cynicism, you're a naive idealist. After all, as Darwin said, we're descended from apes."

Reuben said without looking up from his plate, "Darwin never said that."

Conversation stopped. He felt them turn and look at him but he took his time chewing and swallowing. "What he said was, apes and Homo sapiens are descended from a common ancestor."

And that was all he said throughout the entire meal.

After a moment the conversation continued, but in a lower key. Kane said, "You're the cynic, Tony. You're doing this film because it'll make millions and goose your reputation as a producer."

Tony Quayle said with a little laugh, "Oh, come on,

life's a game, and games are about competition. The script's got everything a good film needs. Conflict, that's the ticket."

The novelist said softly, "Sometimes the greatest conflict is within."

"It's pace that makes a good film," Nat Reybuhr said.

"You are right, my friend," Armisted Whatley said with irony. "Like certain species of insects, we are creatures drawn to colorful fast-moving objects." He wiped his lips with his napkin.

The chair beside Reuben remained unoccupied throughout the meal.

12

Reuben came down hard on the gas, and the old Cadillac gulped once and charged out on the highway in front of a semi. The trucker sat on his horn but lagged behind on the hill past the opera, closed now till next season.

When the Caddy topped the hill, Santa Fe came into view below with the high Sandias powder blue in the distance and the closer hills purple.

The big car had come in handy. He'd driven it around the back of the house and piled it high with his things and laid the old wooden easel across the top of the seats.

Well, he asked himself, what do you think of them?

Kane's trying to kill himself eating. The Spaniard's an old fake. And Zoe McNaire's a little nuts.

What about the scriptwriter?

He's probably gay.

He took the Old Taos Highway cutoff and drifted down toward the Paseo thinking about Tony Quayle. The man now struck him as an enigma. He could play anything convincingly but himself. As himself he seemed at pains to hide some private agenda.

He'd seen him on the New York stage as Richard III, Shakespeare's villain (though apparently Shakespeare had looked into that no further than Hollingshed, who'd looked no further than Thomas More, both of them wrong and a good man maligned). And he'd seen clips of Quayle's first role, Lear's Fool, when he'd stolen the stage from Burton.

For roles as disparate as that it didn't take an actor, it took a chameleon.

Margarite Barbon looked driven. Her sex life was probably nonexistent.

What about yours? he asked himself, not without irony.

The honeymoon couple was a joke. That young guy obviously married the old gal for her money.

Then he told himself: Forget it, you've had it with that bunch, you're getting out. All you've got to do is return the Porsche and you'll have your life back.

He swerved up the Garcia hill to the compound he called home, and stopped long enough to unload his things and stack them under the *portal* in front of his pad. Then he proceeded to Perdita Waldheimer's where he put the Caddy in the garage and drove off in the Porsche.

On his way back to Tesuque, he stopped at the compound to let Magda know he was coming home. He found her in her den of a kitchen hung with garlic and chili *ristras*, the small television turned to a soap opera but her head bent and her bracelets jangling as she worked at the loom. The Siamese cat Gingy—one of the four— glared at him with violet eyes when he eyed the rocker she cozily occupied. He picked her up.

"This cat's cross-eyed."

"She is not," Magda said without looking up, "she's just very focused."

They teased Magda a lot about her cats. There were

also Pussyfoot (an enormous tortoiseshell), Phaedra (an Abyssinian), and Max the Manx.

He settled Gingy on his lap, but she leapt off incensed. The shuttle shot back and forth while Magda listened to his grievances. When he'd got out the last of them, the place seemed unusually quiet.

"Where is everybody?" He was thinking of Tina.

"Gin's gone to Mora. Her grandmother's sick."

He waited. He wasn't going to ask.

"And I guess Tina's asleep," she added.

He eyed her. Was she teasing him? But Tina did make a habit of painting till dawn, using artificial light, which he disapproved, then catching up on her sleep during the day.

"She's been seeing somebody," Magda said softly.

"*Seeing* somebody!"

Magda avoided looking at him, her head piled high with gold curls bent studiously over the loom.

"*Seeing who?*" he demanded more forcefully than he'd intended.

Magda shrugged. Her gold bracelets tinkled like bells as she shot the shuttle. "He's stocky for his height. Wears his hair in braids." She stole a glance at him, but when he looked at her she was blandly adjusting a ratchet.

"So, she's seeing some Indian guy," he said with a little laugh in a voice as light as he could make it.

Magda said, "Maybe he's a relative."

"She ought to be getting her work done!"

The loom started up again. Reuben studied his land-lady, and hoping for more he told her whatever he could think of about the film people. Magda pretended an interest and now and then glanced up with a smile. He snatched looks across the parking lot at Tina's studio.

The door was closed and the blinds drawn. He wondered if she was just sleeping late, as was her habit, or if maybe she wasn't alone in there.

At this time of day? He snorted. But when Magda looked up, he swiped a finger across his nose, pretending he'd sneezed. What with one thing and another, he managed to stay much longer than he'd intended. It was getting late and he was taking his leave and Magda had followed him outside, a sweater of her own design—red and rust and orange and pink—thrown over her shoulders, when a squad car crept into the compound and halted out on the gravel with its motor running.

They watched two officers get out—one tall and Hispanic, the other a short Anglo. The tall one walked toward them.

Puzzled and with a touch of foreboding, Reuben said yeah, that was Tony Quayle's Porsche, and sure it was okay if they looked through his stuff.

The Anglo went to Reuben's *portal* while the Spanish one searched the Porsche and checked the ID number. Then the two conferred, and the tall officer consulted the sky and took a round black packet off the back of his belt. Approaching, he said to Reuben, "Looks like we're gonna have to take you in."

The black packet turned out to contain handcuffs.

13

Lieutenant Tito Gonzales was coming down with a cold. He'd already decided to check in and beg off sick when the captain reached him in his car.

"Why me?" he exploded into his handkerchief. "Get a detective on it!"

But the captain said this one was going to be high profile—it was movie people—and he wanted a lieutenant. "You, Tito. Get on out to Tesuque."

"Tesuque! That's the county! Why'n't you call the sheriff!"

Enlisting his endless patience, the captain explained that hikers were lost in the Jemez, and the sheriff and his staff had joined the search.

So Tito turned around and headed out, taking his time, on the winding Tesuque road full of elbows, thinking: They used to keep cows and goats in their yards out here. Now it's *fashionable*. Expensive as the devil. Why'd anybody want to live in a canyon? Sun comes up late, goes down early. Used to make sense because of the stream, back when nobody had a faucet you could just turn on. Water was still damn valuable. Hell, so many moving in—New York, Califor-ni-ay—putting in lawns for Crissake, they'd soon drain the aquifers. In twenty-thirty years Santa Fe'll

be another Mesa Verde. Why the Indians left those towns
they built in the cliffs, the water gave out.

He arrived at the house shortly after the sergeant had
secured the crime scene and the techs had gone to work.
Some movie mogul's house. Hey, he'd seen the guy in
something. So look around, remember stuff to tell the
little wife. She'd get off on it. She'd listen to him for a
minute and quit tending to the babies. These days it was
the babies got all her attention. He'd asked her, "So
why'd you marry me anyway?"

She'd tugged an end of his mustache. "I wanted pretty
babies."

That got him. She thought he was pretty. He'd ducked
to look at himself in the mirror and stroked his cheek and
smoothed his hair and shrugged.

When he entered the Tesuque house the first thing he
saw was Money. Place reeked of it—furnishings, the size
of the rooms, artwork, even the panoramic views. So
what'd you expect? he asked himself. The second thing
he noticed was how the people grouped themselves. He
didn't know who they were yet, but a good-looking
young thing weeped on the sofa and a fat man had a hand
over hers; a redheaded woman sat at the bar with a
cadaverous long-hair, both of them clutching drinks; the
vaguely familiar man he took to be the homeowner
rushed to greet him from what was probably the kitchen.
Through the swinging door a good-looking Spanish
woman in an apron peered out the fraction of a second
before the door swung to. And out there on the patio, two
black guys and what appeared to be a very short man
with a beard.

The only one of them all by himself—tall, lanky—
stood with his back to the room looking out the window

at the mountain. Two officers watched over them with their hands behind their backs—one at the arch to the hall, the other at the sliding doors to the patio.

The detective was there and briefed him—a good-looking broad, she thought he was a male chauvinist pig. Pig, maybe. On the rest, the jury was still out. Detective Paula Bianci—trim, decisive, black hair pulled smoothly back and held in a clip. She had on gray slacks and a darker gray turtleneck under a red wool vest covered with Mimbres figures, her only jewelry a pair of turquoise stud earrings. He liked her style. Detective Bianci and Lieutenant Gonzales made it a habit to steer clear of each other whenever possible. She thought he thought the proper status of women in the department was meter maid. He thought if he didn't watch out she'd slap him with sexual harassment at the least provocation.

She briefed him about a missing necklace, a missing Porsche, and a missing caretaker. The caretaker was gone with all his things, the apartment absolutely cleaned out. She'd gotten a name and address and dispatched a squad car.

So he already had his suspect. He'd put this one away in a hurry. Open-and-shut case, he'd tell the captain. Victim woke up and surprised him trying to get at the necklace. In a panic he killed her, snatched the necklace, and ran—in Anthony Quayle's Porsche. Clearly the guy's an amateur.

The detective walked him through the crime scene— old gal still there on the bed with her makeup smeared. That got to him, he must be getting old. One of the techs made a joke about Miss America 1910 he pretended not to hear. In spite of his cold he was noticing things, getting into it. That pillow. Why was it on the floor? If it hadn't been for that pillow, nobody would have thought murder. They had a careless killer here. Good.

He looked at the old girl again, lying there with her wig askew. About a hundred years old. The wig, all that makeup—foundation, lipstick, blush, eyebrow pencil, eyeliner—face repeated on that pillow. Christ, looking at it he had the impression he could see her minus the age and wrinkles, staring back at him, challenging. Why the hell would anybody . . . ? He'd like to wring the caretaker's neck.

The captain said, Don't put your feelings in the mix, Gonzales. But the captain had to admit Lieutenant Gonzales was a bulldog when he got his dander up.

The detective pointed out scratches on the victim's neck and throat. "We presumed from missing necklaces," she said, "and the husband confirmed."

She filled him in on what they knew. The old lady felt faint, was wheeled to one of the bedrooms by her husband, who claimed to have brought her the glass of water she'd requested, then skipped lunch and gone for a stroll in the hills. After lunch Margarite Barbon had returned to her guest bedroom, tiptoed in to keep from waking Dame Charlotte, retrieved her cigarettes, then glancing at the sleeper realized something was wrong. The old lady was lying on the bed with her eyes open staring at the ceiling. When Barbon spoke to her, she failed to respond. Her oxygen tubes lay halfway across the room on the floor alongside that pillow.

The lieutenant wandered around the house for a quarter hour, stopping at the dining room table to survey the cold leavings of the meal.

"Get somebody to map out where everybody sat," he

told the detective. "Collect the glasses and label 'em and get 'em to the lab for prints."

She nodded.

"Okay," he said with a sigh, looking toward the patio where she'd asked them all to wait, "might as well bring 'em on. Start with the boy husband."

Detective Bianci consulted her notebook. "Simon Blakemore," she told him.

The lieutenant sauntered to the kitchen for a glass of water and returned with it to the living room. Seeing Simon Blakemore there on the couch gave him a turn. They'd told him the groom was still in his twenties, they hadn't told him he was a black man. He'd been the one alone over by the window. So, had the others been allowing him his moment of grief, or avoiding him because they thought he was the murderer?

Light-skinned, with precise features, in navy blue suit pants and pale blue dress shirt with the sleeves rolled, Blakemore sat with his arms along the back of the couch and one long leg balanced across the other knee. The lieutenant glanced at the shoe. Tassel loafer, not much good for walking in the hills, but covered with dust over a high shine.

"My condolences."

Blakemore looked surprised. "Thank you."

Then he repeated to the lieutenant everything he'd told the detective.

"How long did you walk up there?" The lieutenant hiked his head toward the hills.

"I don't know, maybe a little over an hour."

"See anybody, anybody see you?"

"No."

"About the missing jewelry."

"One of the necklaces was valuable."

"Could you describe it?"

Blakemore looked annoyed. "I described it for the detective." But then he added, "Ornate gold, heavy, with five large square emeralds, maybe ten carats each."

Tito whistled. "Know its value?"

"I'd say at least a couple million."

The lieutenant's eyebrows shot up. He brought them under control. "When you left her she was still alive." He watched Blakemore's arms come off the back of the couch, and hurried on, "And you returned after the death had been discovered."

Blakemore nodded—warily, Tito thought. "Yes. Kane had called 911 but they hadn't yet arrived. The director had started CPR."

"And that was continuing."

Another nod. "Dame Charlotte was clearly dead, but somebody thought the law requires CPR be continued till the ambulance unit arrives. Datrey Moss was spelling her."

Fancy guy, the husband; everything about him, those clothes. He even spoke with a fancy accent.

"You must of been pretty shocked," the lieutenant said, biding his time, watching the man's reactions.

"Her death came as no shock. Dame Charlotte was in poor health and she'd been warned against making a trip to this altitude. It was the manner of her death that was shocking."

"I'm told you'd been married only a short time."

The bridegroom leaned forward, hung his arms off his knees, and looked at the floor. "We were married last Wednesday." Expressionless, the groom met his eyes.

Tito unnecessarily consulted the date on his watch.

* * *

Since the lieutenant had seen Anthony Quayle in some movie or other, the man had aged, and his complexion wasn't good, but maybe that was shock.

"I'm confused why this very old lady in bad health would travel all this way against her doctor's orders to go over a contract."

"Well, actually," Quayle said, "she came to Santa Fe to visit an old friend. We learned from her legal representative, a judge in Montego Bay, that she'd be in Santa Fe. It was a serendipitous turn of events."

Yeah, Tito thought, how much did you have to pay the judge? "Could you tell me your whereabouts between the end of the meeting and lunch? Just to get everybody placed," he added.

Anthony Quayle's foot, on the leg across his knee, began to jiggle.

"I went to the kitchen to see that the wine was chilled. Then I walked up to that outcropping behind the house—" he pointed "—and waited for lunch."

"Didn't feel like talking to your guests."

"The meeting had been trying."

Tito nodded. "Lotta money involved."

"Quite."

"The detective tells me there was a disturbance out here about a month ago. Somebody tryina break in?"

"Oh, no, it was nothing. Nobody arrested. No charges brought."

Tito was looking at that foot. The foot rested.

"How come all these people are here?"

The producer smiled. "It's just a pit stop on our way to Jamaica. We'll be filming there. I thought maybe the—

ah—sheer weight of these people's reputations might help sway the lady's decision."

"Did it?"

Quayle chuckled. "I'm afraid not."

"You're on your way to Jamaica but you hadn't yet got permission to use the plantation."

"Quite true. But Dame Charlotte hadn't *refused*, she was just holding us up for a not-so-small fortune."

Tito nodded. "She was rich but she wanted more money." That figured.

"She had us by the balls, Lieutenant. I had no choice but to agree to her terms. And, ah, Lieutenant, I hope this, ah, unfortunate happening won't unduly delay us. We already have flight plans, you see. Our people are already in Montego Bay. We're ready to go and any delay in our schedule would add enormously to production costs."

Tito Gonzales felt the heat rise from his neck to his face. The captain said, Hold on to that temper, Gonzales, it's got you in trouble more than once.

He looked down and flicked an imaginary speck off his tie. "You were alone up by that pinnacle?"

"Yes, but in plain sight of anybody in the house who happened to look."

Know of anybody who looked?

Watch your manners, Gonzales, the captain said, not everybody at a crime scene is a criminal.

Next, the housekeeper, an uncommonly good-looking woman.

"I was in the kitchen getting ready to serve. After he checked the wine, Mr. Quayle walked up to that rock finger. He was there the whole time. He only came down for lunch."

"You were getting lunch ready but you kept an eye on him up there. Unh-hunh."

She looked at him noncommittally.

So the host had his alibi. The lieutenant looked at his notebook. "Know somebody named Ezekiel Pacheco? Relative of yours?"

"Ezekiel is my husband."

The lieutenant's chin went up. "He caused a disturbance here about a month ago." He pretended to consult his notebook. "That'd be, uh, early October. What was that about?"

She sat primly on the couch with her knees together and her eyes lowered, giving him an opportunity to study her. Dark hair pulled severely back and braided around her head, perfect complexion, the kind of features he associated with portraits in museums. When she looked up he appreciated her eyes, large and dark under perfectly arched brows.

"Says here he created quite a ruckus."

"Ezekiel drinks," she said.

"Ah." He nodded.

"He's sometimes difficult when he drinks."

"A mean drunk, huh. And Ezekiel was drinking that October night?"

"He was upset."

The lieutenant got out his handkerchief and applied it to his nose. He took his time folding it back into his pocket. These little interruptions sometimes worked.

"He doesn't like me working away from home," she said, just as annoyed as if he'd asked. The eyes flashed up at him. "But I must work! I have a son at the university!"

The lieutenant nodded sympathetically. Linda was

already after him about some kind of savings program for the babies. "Your home's in Española?"

"Yes."

"But sometimes you stay here."

"When Mr. Quayle is in residence I do all the cooking," she said with a touch of defiance. "If he entertains I have to remain here late. If the road is iced I stay over."

Aha. Ice in October. "And Ezekiel doesn't like that."

Eyes down again. "No."

"So he had a few and caused a disturbance."

Her eyes came up. She studied him. She was withholding something. He looked back, wondering about her relationship to her employer.

Okay, he had to consider her as a possible. Good-looking woman like that, classy gold and emerald necklace. But murder for it? Only if the old girl woke up and caught her taking the damn thing. Pillow'd be the weapon of choice in that case, wouldn't it?

But somebody would have seen her if she'd left the kitchen and crossed the patio or the living room to the bedroom wing.

On the other hand, in his experience servants tended to be invisible to the rich, they just faded into the landscape. But even if she had it—and no matter how incredible it would look on her, the woman could never wear it, she didn't move in such circles—if she was the one and had hidden it somewhere in the house, they'd find it. His men were turning the place upside down.

But nah—the least little shake of his head, and she looked at him questioningly—she didn't strike him as the type, and he already had his suspect.

He listened with half an ear to the Jamaican novelist. Datrey Moss had spent half of those twenty minutes before lunch walking in the arroyo with Zoe McNaire. "I was just reassuring her, telling her she'll make a great Esme. The rest of the time I was in Whatley's room, drinking a little toast with him to the signing."

"Jamaican rum?"

The novelist smiled. "You are right, Lieutenant."

The actress told the same tale—neither had seen anybody approach the house or leave by the front door—and after leaving Datrey Moss, she'd gone to the kitchen for a drink of water. He'd have to recheck with the housekeeper on that.

Señor Ribera had been sunning himself in a deck chair on the patio. Branwell Kane had been snoozing on the other side of the pool, waiting to put his belly up to the trough. They corroborated each other's whereabouts.

Kane said, "I heard voices raised in anger inside the house, Lieutenant."

The lieutenant looked up. "Any idea whose?"

Kane shrugged and shook his head. "It was a man and a woman. That's all I can tell you."

Nat Reybuhr and the director had gone to Reybuhr's bedroom to go over certain changes in the script.

"Your bedroom—where's that, exactly?"

"At the end of the corridor," Reybuhr said.

"Past where the lady was resting?"

"Yes."

"Hear anything?"

Reybuhr shook his head. "Nothing."

"See anybody in the hall?"

Reybuhr shrugged. "I can't tell you anything, Lieutenant. We were pretty caught up in the discussion."

"Arguing?"

"Well, yes, actually we were."

"Didn't notice anything when you passed the—uh—lady's door on your way to lunch?"

"No."

When he questioned her, the director told the same story.

Incredible. The lieutenant stood up and stretched. He'd got the feeling these people didn't much like each other—except the host and his housekeeper, who maybe liked each other more than they were saying—but once they needed an alibi, everybody's palsying around, not one of them with a minute unaccounted for. In any murder investigation he'd ever run, there'd be at least one suspect all by himself reading a book or watching the tube or taking a walk. Any other time he'd be suspicious. But this time he had his suspect. He wondered if they'd picked him up.

The OMI hadn't arrived. It was getting late. He'd finish up in a few minutes and be out of here. He sat down again when Armisted Whatley came in. He'd purposely saved the Jamaica historian till last.

Before his celebration drink with Moss, Armisted Whatley said he'd spent ten minutes talking long distance to Jamaica on the extension in his room. "I wanted my office to know the contract had been signed and film people were on their way. Public relations, Lieutenant."

He gave the detective a look. She nodded. She would check with the phone company.

He contemplated the Jamaican across the black rock coffee table. He'd saved Whatley till last because he'd picked up that the man enjoyed the sound of his own voice and information might inadvertently surface.

"So, the victim's from Jamaica." He reminded himself to see that the embassy was notified.

"Ah, yes," Whatley said, "this is but another tragedy in the island's long and *violent* history. Sad, when you think of it."

With that strange high breaking voice, the man seemed to Tito Gonzales inappropriately amused.

"Cristopher Columbus thought Jamaica the most *beauti*ful of the islands, and yet it has had a most *vio*lent past."

"That right?"

The historian was very tall and very black and very self-assured under that silver skullcap of hair.

"Yes, the victim was from Jamaica, though rich plantation owners often choose to live most of the year elsewhere."

"This one do that?"

"Uh, no, I don't believe so."

Ordinarily everything would point to the husband, but why would he be in such a hurry to kill the old lady? She was already on her last leg.

He cursed the tardy OMI. There were three or four Officers of Medical Investigation for each county but sometimes one was hard to find.

The missing gold and emerald necklace, along with all the other gold strands, was—according to Detective Bianci—the first thing the husband had noticed. If he'd done the deed, why mention the jewelry at all? And why take it in the first place? If he was the heir it was already his the minute the old lady croaked.

Lt. Gonzales shot his sleeve and looked at his watch. He wouldn't wait much longer.

The historian was saying, "Actually, except for Port *Royale*, Turtle Bay Plantation has perhaps the *most* violent history in the islands. Of course in Spanish times, it was not a plan-*teh*-tion, but a rancheria. But the Spanish owners weren't farmers. The Spanish were only interested in digging for gold."

"Gold, huh."

Outside, a uniformed officer put his nose to the window, shaded his eyes, peered in at them, and went away.

"Not that they found any on the island. But a great many Indians *died* in those barren mines."

The lieutenant glanced impatiently down the hall toward where the body still lay and the crime scene techs were finishing up with the videoing and dusting for latents.

"They were Arawaks, a peaceful people, extinct soon after the Spanish landed."

"That a fact."

He was aware of flashes down the hall. The still photographer finishing up.

So, okay, everybody with alibis, who does that leave?

It left the missing caretaker.

"It was in *British* times that Turtle Bay became a *real* plan-*teh*-tion," Whatley went on, as if he were used to talking to large audiences. "The place is vast, comprising lands in the mountains, where the crop is coffee, and the original *very* large plot in the hills, where it's mostly spices, and of course the Cockpits."

The lieutenant perked up. "Cockfights?"

Whatley threw back his head and laughed, and the lieutenant stared into the cavern of the Jamaican's healthy pink mouth.

"No-no," Whatley said, "the Cockpits are in the mountains where rain and erosion have exposed the native limestone of the island. The Cockpits are pits and *ceh-ves*, you see, in the limestone, some, they say, leading all the way to the sea. It's a strange country, full of symmetrical domes and star-shaped pits. Because of its strange configurations it's mostly useless land. That's why it was left to the old Maroons. It was their mountain fastness."

Prime him a little, the man ran on like that pink drummer rabbit.

"Black sleh-ves were later imported from the Ivory Coast. In the uprising this film recounts, the owners of the plan-*teh*-tion were massacred in their beds, the fields burned, and the sleh-ves escaped to the hills. Do you know about the Maroons, Lieutenant?"

Damn if the fellow wasn't interrogating *him*.

"I could *easily* be a descendant of one of them."

"You don't say."

"But indeed I do," the Jamaican said. "The Maroons held out up there for years, harassing the plan-*teh*-tions from strongholds in the Cockpit Country."

Tito leaned forward with his arms on his knees and asked confidentially, "Know of anybody had it in for the old girl?"

Woman, said the little wife's voice. Nobody'd told him that when you marry she not only came to live in your house but took up residence in your head. Not enough that she'd ditched his wardrobe, cleaned up his habits, and had him smoking on the back *portal*, when the babies came along and he wouldn't quit the nasty habit, she'd made him double his life insurance.

"But, Lieutenant," the historian was saying in that jocular voice, "don't lawmen always start at the beginning? Don't you always ask who stands to *geh-n* by the death?"

Now the guy was telling him his job. "I was wondering," he said, "if you know of any individual in this house with some prior connection to Jamaica."

Armisted Whatley chuckled and light flashed off his little prissy glasses, obscuring his eyes. "I would not be greh-tly surprised if it turned out *everybody* in this house has some prior connection to Jam-eh-ca."

But when questioned further, the historian grew uncharacteristically vague.

The lieutenant dismissed the man, looked at his watch, and rose to leave. It was then that Detective Bianci came running in to tell him Simon Blakemore had disappeared.

"How the hell could he disappear and the place crawling with cops!"

Detective Bianci flushed. "One minute he was there on the patio with the others, the next minute he was gone, though nobody saw him go."

"Christ!" he exploded. He'd have somebody on the carpet for this, maybe Detective Bianci. If they didn't find Blakemore soon he could bring in the helicopters. It didn't look good—the lady old and rich, husband maybe twenty-five twenty-six years old, married for a few days and probably the heir, and now this disappearance.

He asked how long the man had been gone. A chastened Paula Bianci said she didn't know. And neither, it appeared, did anybody else.

Tito called headquarters for additional men to cover the foothills and was told none were available. He cursed the lost hikers in the Jemez. Outside the window uniformed officers scrambled up the sandstone hills in their black cop shoes. Squad cars cranked up out front. Sirens sounded.

"What the hell's the point of that? Tell them to cut the damn things!"

Then he reminded himself of the missing caretaker and was comforted. He asked if they'd picked him up yet.

The detective told him they had.

That was a relief. "Who is he? Any priors? What's the guy's name?"

When she told him, Tito's mouth opened. "Oh, hell," he muttered, and sank back down on the couch.

"Is something the matter, Lieutenant?"

"Never mind," he said. He pulled himself together and looked up at the mountain. Already up there temperatures dropped below freezing at night. If Simon Blakemore was headed for the mountain in nothing but his shirt and trousers he'd be in plenty of trouble.

14

Police headquarters might be more like a new high school than the grim buildings stained with industrial grime seen on TV cop shows, and the room where they filled out papers reminded him of a principal's office, full of blond wood, but Reuben still felt like a stun gun had hit him.

They'd taken off the handcuffs, and they let him sit stewing at a table in the interrogation room. No scarred and battered table, no little window high up in a door where periodically the accused caught glimpses of an eye peering in at him, never a whole face.

No, the room he was in had clean white walls and a big window with vertical blinds to regulate the Northern New Mexico sun, just now touching the horizon. And more blond wood—a table and three chairs.

He sat facing a dark panel that had to be the one-way glass where they'd no doubt be watching him.

How'd he get in this mess? The next stop would be the Detention Center. They didn't have jails anymore, they had detention centers. This one was off the road to the Country Club. You'd think that was a posh part of town, but think again. In high dry Northern New Mexico, country clubs couldn't just turn on their sprinkler systems at will. This one watered its eighteen-hole golf course with purified effluent from the sewage plant.

So there he'd be, out off Airport Road, so called because the Santa Fe airport—not much of an airport, just for little, mostly private planes—was farther out.

By now the shock had worn off and he was inarticulate with rage. What right had they? All they had to do was talk to Tony Quayle and straighten out this whole mess.

They were letting him cool his heels, but his heels were not cooling. He was ready for battle. But the wind went out of his sails when the door opened and Tina's old friend Tito Gonzales walked in.

But Tito didn't look at him. Just a perfunctory nod as he set a small tape recorder down on the table. "Your name is . . . ?"

Come on, you know me. But he said his name for the tape recorder. He could feel unseen eyes watching from behind the glass panel as he recited his address.

When finally Tito looked at him it was all business. Reuben felt a growing uneasiness, but he told himself Tito was just doing his job.

The lieutenant flipped through his notebook, scanning pages. "Okay, so—your story is, Quayle let you drive his hundred-thousand-dollar sports job whenever you liked." The lieutenant's eyebrows went up skeptically. "Generous guy."

"Yeah," Reuben said. Then for the sake of whoever was behind the glass, he cleared his throat and repeated, "Yes. That way I could drive him to and from the airport whenever he came to town."

Tito nodded. "So how come now Quayle's in Santa Fe you're still driving the Porsche?" The lieutenant leaned on the table and looked him in the eye.

Reuben willed himself not to flinch. "He sent me on an errand."

"Unh-hunh."

"Look, I haven't done anything. I don't know why I'm here."

Tito straightened and turned his back and trailing a finger along the tabletop crossed to the window and stood looking out, fiddling with the blind cord.

Reuben let his elbows slide apart till his chin rested on his knuckles. When they read him his Mirandas, it had seemed like a joke, a simple mistake. But maybe he shouldn't have waived his rights.

"Look, if I'd stolen the Porsche, would I have calmly gone back to the compound and waited to be picked up?"

Tito didn't answer.

The whole thing was unreal. He looked at the glass panel. Show them he knew they were there. Then to get hold of himself he sat up straight, stretched his legs under the table, and crossed his arms over his chest.

The lieutenant turned and leaned against the window-sill, playing with the blind cord. "Try this scenario. You thought you had enough time to go home and pick up your things before you lit out of town in the Porsche."

"Yeah, right. How far would I have got?"

The lieutenant's smile wasn't friendly. "How far'd you have to get? 'Bout as far as a chop shop in Albuquerque."

Chop shop. Reuben flashed on a Chinese restaurant. Then he caught on. "You mean one of those places take stolen cars to pieces in about fifteen minutes and sell the parts?" He'd seen it on *NYPD Blue*.

Tito said, "Look, kid, you can smile or you can wipe it. It's your ass."

That was sobering.

Tito came back and slid a hip onto the edge of the table. "How long've you been employed as caretaker out there?"

"About a month."

"And you just pack up all your stuff and leave without a word to your employer?"

"I was fed up."

"How much was he paying you?"

"None of your business."

"So let's see if I've got it." The lieutenant's smile was menacing. "Apartment, Porsche, salary, but you were fed up."

The guy could be hard as nails. But Reuben told himself it was an act for the benefit of whoever watched behind the glass.

"I tried to talk to Tony Quayle, tell him I was out of there. He was too busy to listen. If you don't believe me, ask him."

Slapping his notebook against his other palm, Tito looked away nodding. "You were just moving back to your pad off Garcia."

"Right."

The lieutenant turned up the sole of his shoe and studied it. "Terrific place compared to the apartment in Tesuque."

"Be it ever so humble . . ."

The lieutenant dropped his foot and leaned over in Reuben's face. "So you packed up all your stuff and left in the Caddy. Suddenly you just didn't want to drive around in the Porsche, is that it? You didn't really stash it out up there in the piñons off the Old Santa Fe Trail intending to pick it up later."

Reuben leaned back away from the lieutenant. They told him when he waived his rights he could stop answering questions at any time. Maybe that time had come.

But if he stopped talking, wouldn't it look like he had something to hide?

"Look, Tito," he said softly so maybe whoever was behind the glass wouldn't hear, "you know me. All you've got to do is ask Anthony Quayle. Or ask Perdita Waldheimer. She'll tell you why I left the Porsche at her place."

"You had prior contact with old lady Saxe-Ogilvy."

Prior contact. He was starting to feel weak, lightheaded. He let his arms fall flat on the table with a thud. "I never saw the lady before this morning. Tony Quayle sent me out there to pick her up and bring her out to Tesuque. That's all I know." And what had the old lady in the wheelchair to do with a stolen automobile?

"And I never *hid* the Porsche." He caught a guilty note in his voice and told himself, Stop being defensive!

He saw Tito glance at the glass panel. "The way it looks," he said, "you stashed the Porsche, returned to Tesuque and packed up the old Caddy, and left your stuff at your pad where you could pick it up later in the sports car and hightail it out of Santa Fe. Only we picked you up instead."

"I'd just taken my stuff *home*! I hadn't had time to unpack! And anyway," he said, "why would I take my stuff home? Why not just transfer it to the Porsche out at the Waldheimer place if I was planning to leave Santa Fe?"

Tito said, "Beats me. You wanna tell me about it?" Then he jotted something in his notebook, sighed, and straightened.

"Look, kid," he said, glancing at the one-way glass, turning his back to it, leaning down, "maybe you oughta stop talking till you see a lawyer."

"Why the hell would I need a lawyer? I haven't *done* anything!"

Tito slid a hip on the table again and glanced smiling at

the one-way glass. There was a little flat mole on his jaw that Reuben had never noticed before. "Listen to what I'm telling you, kid," he said, "you could be in deep shit."

Reuben said, "You don't actually think I *stole* that car?"

"Car's the least of your problems, pal."

"I don't know what you're talking about!"

"Well, for starters, there's the Porsche. And from there let's go to what one of the officers found in your paint box up there at Magda's under the portal."

"In my paint box," Reuben repeated, nodding. "What, brushes and rags and tubes of incriminating color?"

"Yeah, all that and a handful of the lady's gold chains—"

Reuben lapsed back limp in his chair.

"—wrapped up in a handkerchief with your initials."

His insides went weak and runny. He looked point-lessly around. Was there a toilet in this place?

"So now I'm also a jewel thief?" His voice was husky. "My mother sent me a half dozen handkerchiefs for my birthday." He felt a quick anger at his mother, as if she'd got him into this mess. He straightened his leg and dug in his pocket. Nothing there but loose change and keys. No handkerchief. "I had the apartment keys in my pocket," he said. "I took them off the key chain and left them in the apartment. I must have dropped the handkerchief." Then he felt guilty for blaming his mother, who had spent all that time embroidering his initials.

"What all am I being held for?"

"Possession of stolen property," the lieutenant said, "for now."

"For now!"

Before, he'd felt angry, misused, misunderstood. Now he was just plain scared.

15

It was dinnertime and Tito Gonzales was hungry, but here he was, way out on the Old Santa Fe Trail. He had to go see the other old gal. The two had been in school together. He smiled and turned on his headlights. Must've been a while back, he thought. Like maybe a hundred years. These thoughts got him as far as the Waldheimer mailbox.

He turned off the Old Santa Fe Trail and wound up through the piñon trees in the gathering dark. He missed daylight savings and at the same time wished they'd leave the damn clocks alone.

Informing the near and dear was his notion of torture. And the job shouldn't have been his anyway, it was usually left to a couple of respectful patrolmen. But the captain repeated "high-profile case" and "leading citizen." Also the lieutenant could kill two birds with one stone. So here he was.

When the old boy let him in, she called out from the living room, "Who is it, Jack?" Then he had to wait while the old boy announced him.

The lieutenant told her the sad news, then hung his head and stood with his hands folded respectfully over his crotch while the old doll's shoulders slumped and her eyes blurred behind her little glasses on a dainty loop of silver chain. She reached up and unpinched them from her nose and reeled them back to the little silver disk pinned to her sweater.

"Oh, my," she said. "I ought not be surprised. She's been in terrible health. And then the flight and the altitude."

The lieutenant shifted his weight uncomfortably and put his hands in his pockets. "Well, uh, ma'am, I'm afraid it wasn't the altitude." She was a pretty little old thing, all dolled up in her matching sweater and slacks, hair like she just got home from the beauty shop.

"Ma'am, we, uh, I'm afraid we suspect your friend may of been murdered."

Perdita Waldheimer gasped. He waited anxiously for the exhale. He looked at the butler and requested a glass of water. The old man raised his eyebrows, then shuffled off in what for him was probably a rush.

Perdita Waldheimer said, "What on earth . . . ?"

The lieutenant explained as much as he could of what had happened, including the missing jewelry. He left out that pillow.

"Was she . . . did she suffer?"

"No, ma'am." Not for long anyway, he thought.

"But who on earth would do such a thing?"

"We don't know yet, ma'am."

Jack came back with the glass of water on a silver tray and offered it disapprovingly to the lieutenant.

"Not me!" Tito hissed, and jabbed a finger toward Perdita.

Old Jack's eyebrows went up. He nodded approvingly and offered her the glass. She took it like an obedient child and held it in both hands on her lap.

"She'd been warned about the trip, but you couldn't

stop Charlotte. She was a daredevil. Once she made up her mind to do a thing, she did it."

Tito let himself down to sit on the hearth. A low, menacing growl came from the shadows of the window seat. Then—he couldn't believe it—a wolf slunk into view with his teeth bared and his hackles up. Tito skidded back till the fire heated his coattails.

"Behave yourself, Nemo," Perdita murmured, dropping a hand beside her chair. The wolf sidled up under the blue-veined hand, and it absently patted the heavy head.

"It's prophetic," she said. "We were just talking about death." She looked hopefully at the lieutenant. "She wanted to know if she died would she return."

What, the old lady wanted to be a ghost?

Perdita said, "She wanted to know about reincarnation, you see."

"Oh. Yeah. Okay."

When he asked about the Porsche left in front of her house, she smiled. "You couldn't expect Charlotte to ride in that little thing, now could you?"

"No, ma'am, I guess . . . So you're saying that's why the driver took them out to Tesuque in your Cadillac."

It confirmed what the suspect had told him about the Porsche, but that didn't explain the gold chains in the paint box, or why Beardboy had whisked away all his belongings without a word to anybody. And though they'd retrieved the Porsche, it didn't clear him of auto theft. When they caught up with him, he still hadn't returned the car to its owner, had he?

But the hundred-thousand-dollar car was peanuts to the missing emeralds. Where were they?

Old Jack came back with a tray of brandy and three snifters. Tito looked at it longingly, but he was on duty.

He watched Old Jack set the tray on a hassock, serve the old lady, and take one for himself. What kind of a servant was that?

Perdita Waldheimer said, "What exactly can I do for you, Lieutenant?"

"Well, ma'am, if I could just look over the lady's— uh—effects."

"Of course," she said. "Jack, show the lieutenant . . ."

So he spent the next quarter hour in one of the bedrooms, rummaging through the dead woman's luggage, fingering a dress, picking up a shoe—the old doll wore these little low heels. He went through a jewelry box holding now only a few sets of earrings, sniffed bottles and jars on the dresser: blush, lipstick, eyebrow pencil, eye shadow. He saw that pillow again, like she was watching.

He thought of his wife Linda. All dressed up and ready to go, he liked to pile up against the head of the bed and watch her slow ritual. First that stuff—wha'd they call it?—had to match the skin. Wha'd they need it for if it matched their skin? Then a little blush. Then eyeliner. She was terrific at eyeliner. And shadow. He thought the whole thing was sexy. Lipstick. Now they brush it on. Used to be, it came in a tube.

In the adjoining room all he did was check on the wheeled suitcase, make sure it was still there—chinos, shirts, bedroom slippers, shaving kit—though he did ask Perdita if the bridegroom had more than one travel case.

"Oh, I don't know. I don't think so," she said.

He told her they needed to know who to phone in Jamaica, who was in charge of the—uh—estate.

"Oh, I'd think that would be Simon," Perdita said. "Where *is* Simon? The poor boy must be in an awful state."

"Yeah," the lieutenant said. "I guess he'd be all broke up. Thing is, we hab'n been able to locate him."

The old lady's eyes went wide. "My goodness!" she said. "If Charlotte was *murdered*, do you think Simon could be in danger?"

16

In the gathering dusk Reuben was taken sullen and handcuffed from the interrogation room to the County Detention Center, a sprawling ersatz adobe with flagpoles out front. The squad car pulled around back and stopped at a big red corrugated metal door, and the driver told a grill that police were at the sally port. "We're bringing in a 1015."

Reuben snorted. "What the hell's a 1015? I'm a person, for Crissake." But he was beginning to feel like something less.

A disembodied voice told the patrolmen to put their weapons in the weapon locker. The driver handed his sidearm to his partner, who got out and came back empty-handed. Then the voice asked if their weapons were secured.

Reuben muttered, "Star Wars."

Without turning the driver said, "A 1015's an adult male."

"Why not just say so?"

The metal door rumbled noisily up and the squad car pulled into a long enclosed drive-through with an identical big red metal door at the other end. Another patrol car was parked ahead of them, nobody in it. The two cops got out, a heavy red metal door in the wall slid aside, and they ushered him into a claustrophobic room with a ticket-booth window behind a stainless steel counter.

Ahead, another prisoner waited with his keepers. He was a heavyset youth in white running pants and a wind-breaker. Apparently the agent at the window wasn't letting them in.

"Bring him bleeding from the hospital, you think we'll take him like that!"

"Hospital released him. It's just his sutures leaking a little."

"What? A stabbing?"

"Yeah."

One leg of the prisoner's running pants was startlingly red around the edges, the blood darker in the middle where it pooled and clotted. Reuben looked up at the young man's face, round and ruddy, topped by close-cropped straw-colored thatch. Expressionless, he looked back at Reuben and their eyes met for a minute.

The man behind the glass sighed. "Okay. Lemme have the papers. Bring him on in. We'll see if the medical officer's satisfied."

Another red metal door slid open. The doors he saw through the booking window were blue. Apparently doors here were all painted primary colors—red, blue, no yellow yet. He watched through the glass as the bleeding prisoner was patted down, his handcuffs removed and handed back to his keepers.

He tried to read the form his own driver was filling out. Arresting Agency. Date. Name. His eye stopped at Felony. *He'd been arrested on a felony!* Had they told him that? He didn't remember. He was feeling increasingly disoriented. The form slid back through the slot and the man behind the glass had to go over it item by item. Then the red door slid open, admitting them. In another life this might have been interesting.

Inside, it was like the lobby of a second-rate hotel. Long desk, industrial carpet. Like the other prisoner, he was patted down and his handcuffs removed and returned to his escorts. He didn't see them leave. He felt abandoned.

Then up at the desk another form. Race. Sex. Birth date. Age. Height. Weight. Hair. Eyes. Scars and marks. Alcoholism? Mental illness? Drug abuse? Diabetes? Epilepsy? He answered questions in a monotone.

The booking agent had on a white shirt with epaulets and some kind of arm patch, dark trousers with a stripe up the side. Like some little off-brand country's naval uniform.

He was told to turn out his pockets.

Keys. But those weren't his, they were the keys to Perdita Waldheimer's Caddy. Startled, he decided to keep quiet about that. He handed them over and wondered how long before they'd be missed. Would Perdita report it? Could it get him in more trouble?

Another form. Everything in triplicate. This could get tedious. On this one things had to be checked off a list:

keys
sunglasses
wristwatch
wallet

He found himself slowly detaching. It was not quite an out-of-body experience, but gratifying. Good. He could go through this shit as an observer. It allowed him to feel superior to these people who had control over him, it allowed him to sign another form and without the slightest sense of loss watch his things taken away.

Next, they took him across the room and stood him up against a height chart. They handed him a number plate and told him to hold it across his chest.

Somewhere—maybe in a philosophy class—he'd learned you always have a choice. He remembered doubting it at the time. So what if he refused? He shrugged and took the number plate, part of him still standing off watching, seeing himself up against the wall holding some damn numbers that would show up forever after on his mug shot.

Only one. No profiles. Then fingerprints. Not a full set. As if they were objects, his keeper pressed the four fingers of his right hand on an ink pad, then held them all down in the biggest square. Next, his thumb. Only his right hand. What if you were left-handed? He found himself focusing on details with absolute clarity.

They told him he could have three phone calls. They pointed to a sign on the wall over the phone about bail bondsmen, then told him no bond could be posted on a felony charge till after the arraignment.

When would that be?

Next business day after the arrest.

It was Friday. That meant Monday. But the booking officer told him, "Now and then they'll do it on Saturday. Maybe you'll be lucky."

Nothing that had happened so far led him to think so. Now were they through with him?

No.

Next, the medical screening.

Another form. More questions. As he answered, the male nurse checked off items. Another list.

Taking any medication?

Allergic to any medication?

On a special diet?

"Yeah," he said. "Lobster and steak."

The nurse ignored him and went on checking.

Ever confined in this correctional facility before?

It wasn't a jail, it wasn't any longer even a detention center: it was a correctional facility.

Venereal disease? Abnormal discharge? TB? Lice?

Christ!

Had he fainted recently? What about a painful condition? Had he taken any substance that could cause withdrawal?

Check. Check. Check.

"How am I doing?" he asked.

The nurse said without looking up, "You think this is fun, try doing it eight hours a day."

Ever attempted suicide?

Ever thought of suicide?

Ever feel someone's controlling your thoughts or actions?

"Yeah," he said, "I've felt that ever since I walked through that door."

Next, the Classification Officer.

He was led to a little room. This time he got to sit down in a chair beside her desk. Good-looking woman in her thirties—suit, blouse, tie. And yet another form. He sighed and dropped his head on top of a stack of papers on her desk.

She looked up startled, then reassured him. "This will be painless."

He straightened and thought he caught a trace of a smile.

More questions. This time he scored points.

Zero for being a New Mexico resident, though he thought it should count for something. Three for being inconsistently employed?

"I'm a painter," he said. "Mostly landscapes."

She circled a zero beside Marketable Skill.

"All this is strictly confidential," she said. "It's just between you and me. None of it will go any further."

So what if it did? Big deal. It wasn't exactly high treason.

"I'm interviewing you," she said, "to get background information in order to place you in the safest and least restrictive housing while you are here." Hair to her shoulders, brown and sort of curly. "I'm not a lawyer, so please don't discuss the facts of your case with me."

Okay.

Education? He got a zero for his B.A.

"Why a zero?"

"The higher the score, the greater the risk," she explained patiently, brown eyes on his face.

"What kind of risk?"

She looked up again with her pencil poised. "This is a multicustody facility."

"Multicustody," he repeated, looking at her.

"That means residents here may be sentenced anywhere from one day to one year, in anything from minimum to maximum security."

"Residents," he said with a smile.

"Right." She looked back down at the form. "Also, we want to protect residents from threats. At risk are child molesters, homosexuals, potential suicides . . ."

More questions. Military service? Next of kin? Mental health? Alcohol abuse? Drug abuse? She watched him carefully while he addressed himself to these, assessing, he thought, the truth of his answers. Then she turned the sheet over. He sighed. There was more.

Felony, ten points. But only three for the type of offense: nonviolent.

No prior escapes. No sexual variance. Again no suicide history.

Then came Stress Indicators.

Incarceration
Divorce
Marital Separation
Job Loss

He got sixty-three points for Incarceration. Right, he found incarceration pretty unsettling. He examined his state of detachment and found himself still coldly calm.

The Classification Officer totaled up his score and wrote it down, but he couldn't see it.

"How'd I do?"

No smiles.

Then in a room off the booking room his cool detachment deserted him. He was stripped. Overwhelmed by hopeless rage, he shouted, "Get your goddam hands . . ." He put up his arms and backed away from them.

"Look," a Sailor Suit said patiently, keeping his distance, "we didn't arrest you. Be mad at the police, if you want to be mad. We're just doing our job."

Backed up naked against the wall he said, "I want to make a phone call!"

"In a minute," Sailor Suit said. "Look, man, anger won't help you here, but it could get you a higher security. You wouldn't like that."

"I want to make a phone call!" Still warding them off.

"In a minute."

He wilted. The voice of detachment said to him, Just go along with it. He took some deep breaths, straightened up, and smiled grimly while submitting to the humiliation. Fingers through his hair. His mouth and ears explored.

Then, "Squat," Sailor Suit said.

He hesitated, freezing the smile. "You get off on this?"

Sailor Suit said, "How original."

He rendered himself numb again. He squatted. They checked his ass. He wanted to lash out, hit something hard—one, two—with his fists. But ashamed he dropped his head.

They gave him a brown cotton outfit—pants and top. They examined his Nikes and let him keep them and his underwear.

He said again, "I want to make a phone call."

They obligingly led him out to the phone on the wall in the reception room now noisy with cops and prisoners. He thought for a minute, then ran his hand through his hair and dialed the Tesuque number.

The housekeeper answered. He put his hand over the phone to shut out the sounds and asked to speak to Quayle.

"Who may I say is calling?"

He hesitated. "Tell him his agent," he lied.

Quayle came to the phone. "Yeah, Peter?"

"It's me," he said. "Reuben."

Silence at the other end.

He rushed on. "Look, I've been arrested. You've got to tell them I didn't steal the Porsche."

More silence. Then, "Well, but look here, old chap.

We've had a murder here at the house. The police looked for you but you were gone."

A murder. A spot between his nipples went suddenly cold, as if he'd swallowed ice and it had lodged there. "I'd been chauffeuring your friends around," he said as calmly as he could. "I'd gone to return the Caddy. The old lady wouldn't ride in the Porsche. That's where I was!"

"Yes, and I really do appreciate . . . but, don't you see, when they found some of the old girl's jewelry in your box . . ."

"Dame Charlotte? Is that who was murdered?"

More silence. "Hold on a minute, will you," Tony Quayle said. "I've got a call waiting."

A click and Reuben waited for a long time. His jailer came up and touched his elbow. He shook him off. Then finally the phone clicked again.

"Hello? Tony? Hello hello!" But the dial signal came on. Quayle had hung up on him.

"Bastard." He slammed his fist into the wall beside him, then put his forehead against it. And there he remained till they came for him. He'd wasted one of his three calls. He felt like hoarding the others.

He expected a cell in a tiered cellblock with bars, bunks, the works. He felt cheated when it turned out the cell was right there off the lobby, behind one of the numbered doors in primary blue.

It was bigger than he'd expected. Nothing in it but a toilet and sink, and over against the wall a stack of mats on the floor.

His jailer didn't look at him. "You'll be in here overnight."

"Then what? I can go home?"

His jailer twisted his lips with a look that said Please and pointed to the mats. "You can keep all the mattresses."

What, they weren't busy, didn't need them all? They were a little like exercise mats, only pink, and tufted.

The door closed. The lock slid in place. A cell with bars would be better than this, with maybe some sounds down the hall, a cough or a laugh, voices. Right outside was the busy booking office, but this room they'd put him in seemed soundproof.

Cursing, he slung the thin mats one-by-one on top of each other, then threw himself down on them and curled to the wall. After a while they brought him dinner in a Styrofoam box—chicken-fried steak, mashed potatoes, peas. A slab of bread, a cup of coffee.

The night that followed was endless. Sometime in the middle of it he got up and unloaded one of the mats on the floor and did yoga for an hour, ending with a long headstand in the corner. Then ten series of push-ups. He ran in place till he was in a heavy sweat, and dropped finally onto the stack of mats.

Still sleep eluded him. He was alone, in solitary, his detachment gone and emotions rushing into the vacuum left behind. What was this, some kind of existential trial? He thought of Kafka and his mouth twisted into an ironic little smile. Next would he turn into a cockroach?

Come on, said the voice of reason, get a grip.

But where this morning he'd felt lousy about himself because he was being used, tonight he was a mug with a number across his chest.

17

The story was on the front page of Saturday's *New Mexican* with pictures of the Tesuque house and what looked like publicity shots from the paper's morgue of Tony Quayle, Zoe McNaire, and a much younger Branwell Kane. The story recounted the murder and robbery, and said the police had arrested one suspect and were conducting a search for another. Santa Feans in the northeast stood outside in their yards, arms crossed under their sweaters, looking up at police helicopters swinging out over the foothills.

With the help of the pince-nez on the end of her nose and a hand-held magnifying glass, Perdita Waldheimer read the story. She was gratified that they'd picked up a suspect but she was worried sick about Simon. Where could he be? She knew he'd have endless details to attend to, but she had expected to hear from him long before now.

The wolf brushed against her leg, and the golden eyes looked up at her. She bent and looked at him. "Why so worried, Nemo?"

And answered herself, "The wolf feels things."

She told herself Charlotte had known she hadn't long to live. She shouldn't have made this trip, but Charlotte was always one to challenge the gods. Perdita gripped her wadded handkerchief.

She supposed Charlotte would be flown back to Jamaica for burial. Then she thought *autopsy*, and wilted in her chair. It seemed such a violation of the body.

18

The next thing Reuben knew, it was morning, and the electronic door was sliding open.

"Okay, here we go." Another Sailor Suit.

What now?

He was ushered down a long hall smelling of bacon and coffee. At the end of it a handball court, inmates in brown suits like his already hard at play. A weight room on his left. They'd disguised the place as a goddam sports complex. After his solitary night it was a relief to see people.

Under a sign at the end of the hall that said Medium Security, uniformed guards watched in a glassed-in room like the bridge of a ship.

Then into the "dayroom" with heavy metal tables and benches bolted to the concrete floor, a guy in there twiddling dials on a television set.

One wall of the room was glass—or maybe plastic—and on the other side of it prisoners bounced around the handball court. From this angle he could see the garish mural on the opposite wall. High up over the handball court, a see-through ceiling of maybe Plexiglas with wire in it.

This was a jail? Come on. It smelled like a locker

room. Then he saw the coiled razor wire up there on the roof, framing the sky.

On the other side of the dayroom, cells. No bars, just metal doors again. The cell he was taken to was maybe eight by ten with a white ceramic toilet and sink, a set of metal bunks painted institutional brown, a very small desk against the wall, and a high shelf for—what? his toothbrush? He didn't have a toothbrush, but he'd been told there was a commissary.

A man lay on his back on the top bunk with his arms crossed over his chest. Reuben couldn't see his face.

The door behind him stayed open. The jailer was gone. What, no locks? He flipped over the lower bunk's two-inch mattress and threw himself down.

How the devil had this happened to him?

It all started that morning on the bike trail when he ran into (almost literally) the aging film star. Do a goddam man a goddam favor.

He had two phone calls left. He ought to call Magda. She'd be worried sick. Who else, Tina? What could he say to her? But the idea of contact with somebody outside was a comfort. For now, however, he was hungry.

"When do they feed?" he said.

A voice overhead said, "Huh?"

"When do we get breakfast?"

"Pretty soon now."

"I smelled bacon and coffee. That for us or our keepers?"

"They feed pretty good here," said the voice from the upper bunk. "What're you in for?"

Reuben looked at the bottom of the bunk overhead. "Car theft, I guess," he muttered. "But I'm innocent."

A chuckle. "Yeah, man."

No sense in arguing the point. "What about you?"

"Cutting."

Cutting. What did that mean? "You mean you . . ."

"Hacked, man. Sliced!"

"Who . . ."

"Her husband."

"Oh.

"It was self-defense. He would of killed me."

It was Reuben's turn to chuckle.

His cell-mate rolled over and peered down at him. He was either Pueblo or Navajo.

"Johnny Cordova," he said, and dropped a hand.

Pueblo.

"Reuben." He reached up. They shook.

A Sailor Suit he hadn't seen before pushed a trolly into the dayroom. Breakfast. Men came out of the cells. The jailer opened each Styrofoam box and checked its contents before he passed it out.

What, one of the cooks might be smuggling in a file?

Some "residents" sat at the tables. Others took the food back to their cells. There was a kid's cartoon on the TV—a rabbit skidding around a corner. Johnny Cordova headed back to the cell and Reuben followed. They sat together on the lower bunk and wolfed down stacks of pancakes with sides of bacon and eggs.

"What kind of car?" Johnny Cordova asked, wiping his chin.

"A Porsche 911."

Johnny Cordova swallowed his biscuit and whistled. He was maybe a little older than Reuben. Smooth brown face, wide-set eyes, cropped, spiky hair. Expression: amused. When the guard had taken away their Styrofoam and plastic, Reuben piled up against the head of the bunk and Johnny Cordova sat on the desk with his feet dangling. The canvas slippers he had on looked like jail issue. "Whose Porsche was it?"

So Reuben told him the story.

Throughout the telling, the Indian's smile broadened. "Man," he said when he'd heard it all, "you don't get it, do you? This rich guy makes you an offer you can't refuse—apartment, wages, a Porsche thrown in. Then what? A killing and a theft and the victim's valuables found in your stuff, wrapped up for good measure in your *pañuelo*."

Johnny Cordova shook his head. "Man, *think* about that! You not *thinking*!"

Reuben stared at his cell-mate. Then he rolled his head back and touched the top of it to the wall behind him.

"Christ!" he said. "I've been set up!"

"Now you cooking."

"How could I have been so stupid!?"

The Indian laughed. "Maybe you led a sheltered life."

19

When the wolf howled, Perdita woke instantly and sat
up in bed. The women who cooked and cleaned for her
went home at night. There was only herself and Jack in
the house, and Jack was older than she was. He was also
deaf, and he slept at the back of the house.

Nemo howled again. Usually he slept beside her bed,
but she could tell he was downstairs, just inside the front
door. She slid open her night table drawer and drew out
the little derringer Charley had given her years ago, when
she was hardly more than a girl. It was a pretty nickel-
plated pearl-handled thing, and she kept it always loaded
with small snub-nosed bullets, all but the first round,
which was a blank. With the blank, she could scare off an
intruder. If he didn't scare there was always the second
bullet.

She heard the key turn in the lock downstairs. She
heard the door creak open. Then she knew without
hearing his footsteps that he was mounting the stairs
because the wolf's nails clicked on the parquet steps as
he followed the intruder, who would be no stranger. A
stranger's throat would have been torn out by now.

There in the dark lit only by the cold light of the moon,
sitting up small in her big bed, Perdita saw the white of

her bedroom door shoved inward to disclose a dark panel of hall beyond.

Then she was sure she knew her visitor, though snatched from sleep like that, and without her glasses, she saw hardly more than an indistinct shape at the foot of her bed.

"Simon!" she said. "I've been expecting you."

20

Sunday. Middle of the afternoon. Tito moved around the big living room, feeling the Spanish woman's watchful eyes. A real beauty, he couldn't blame Quayle if he . . . But how'd he feel if he was Ezekiel?

"Gracias," he said. "I won't be needing you." The woman faded into another part of the house.

He'd driven out here in spite of the traffic. Too many people coming to Santa Fe. He'd like to roll up the highways and present them as a gift to Arizona.

But probably the Indians thought something like that when his Spanish forebears came. Maybe they'd wanted to roll up the wagon trails and present them to the Comanches.

Hands in pockets, he sauntered down the hall. It irked him that he hadn't a shred of evidence to hold a one of them. He'd had to let the whole kit and kaboodle leave the country. Hell, they'd counted on that contract. They had to have it and would have paid anything to get it. They'd already made their travel arrangements, and their whole staff was on the island checking locations, signing up extras, waiting for the trailers to move into place, everything ready to go. But they wouldn't be gone forever. They'd be back.

"Anthony Quayle," Linda had said on the other side of his newspaper at breakfast. "To think! Right here in The City Different." She laughed at that city different crap. She'd lived here all her life. If it was different she hadn't known it.

"You actually questioned Zoe McNaire?"

"Unh-hunh."

"I read she ran away from home as a kid and lived on the streets."

"Umm." He shuffled pages and, refolding, smiled across at her.

"You're not listening."

He wiped off the smile and put on an interested look. "Where'd you read that?"

"At the checkout counter."

"Oh." He nodded sagely and copped a look at the sports page.

"But she got on *Oprah* and refuted it. She said Oprah was her role model, she couldn't thank her enough."

She dented the top of his newspaper with her fork. "I read where Quayle left an English wife when he came to this country."

"Huh!" he grunted, putting emphasis on it, and smiled. "Read that at the checkout, too?"

"It was Supercuts," she said. "Where else would I get any reading done?"

That was a complaint: he didn't spell her enough with the babies. He ducked back behind the paper.

"I think there was a picture, a sort of dowdy woman, but maybe that's just English."

His Linda was pretty classy herself—lap swims, aerobics. She never came to the breakfast table in a shapeless old bathrobe or her hair in curlers. He seldom grumbled about following her up front in church, which reminded him, it was time to get out of here.

"How does he look these days, Branwell Kane? I've seen all his old movies. He was a whole lot better than James Dean. For my taste, James Dean overacted."

"Um." She was an expert on the movies. She'd taken a film class at the community college.

She started clearing. "We'd better be getting dressed."

Time to look at his watch. "Jesus!" Big surprise. "Can't make it to church, hon, gotta work." Scrambling up, knocking over his chair and catching it.

She gave him a look, she was onto him. He was hurt. This time, he argued to himself, it was the truth.

The lieutenant's murder cases had mostly been bar fights, domestic brawls, and one he didn't like thinking about—a young woman's decomposing body under a piñon tree out in the sage beyond Solana. He knew who the killer was, but no way to pin it on him. Not yet, but he'd get the creep. A boyfriend she'd told good-bye who refused to get lost. Stalked her for months. She took out a restraining order. Fat lot of good that did.

As he wandered through the Tesuque house the sound of a helicopter grew louder over the mountain, but the lieutenant doubted Blakemore was still out there.

He wasn't sure what he was doing here. The crime scene techs hadn't come up with anything. He leaned against the doorframe surveying the murder bedroom. He could still see the old girl's face on that pillow on the floor, her own personal Shroud of Turin. The vision nagged. In the eyeliner and rouge and lipstick he could still see her looking at him like she was trying to tell him something.

He'd alerted American Airlines to be on the lookout for Simon Blakemore in the unlikely event he got to

Albuquerque and tried to use his return ticket to Jamaica. And on the off chance he made it out of Albuquerque, they'd also be looking for him at Dallas–Ft. Worth.

He wandered around the house for half an hour. When he got back to his office he learned that a couple driving from Denver to El Paso had stopped in Socorro to contact the State Police. They'd heard on their car radio about the search for a murder suspect. Said they'd been approached by a young black man at a filling station outside of Santa Fe, who'd asked for a ride into town. Said he'd locked his keys in his car and had to get back to his hotel to pick up his spares.

This happened Saturday night. Tito muttered, "Damn."

After they'd dropped him off at the Hilton they drove on to Albuquerque and spent the day visiting relatives. They'd only heard of the search when they turned on their car radio somewhere between Belen and Los Lunas.

Then a call was put through to the lieutenant from a young Denver businessman named Polo Prentiss, who'd spent the weekend in the Indian casinos between Santa Fe and Taos. Said he'd just finished fueling his Cessna at the Santa Fe airport, ready to fly home to Colorado Springs, when a young guy carrying a single piece of luggage ran toward him waving.

Polo Prentiss paused to see what the fellow wanted. If he wanted to hitch a ride to Colorado Springs, he'd let him pay for the gas, help make up his gambling losses. But the guy wasn't going to Colorado Springs. He wanted a ride to El Paso. Polo was already shaking his head when the guy set down his suitcase and drew an impressive sheaf of bills from his wallet.

Already resigned to the worst-case scenario, Tito made a few phone calls and learned that someone fitting the suspect's description had boarded American Flight 1742 bound from El Paso with a quick connection to Miami. By the time he hung up, the Miami flight had landed in Montego Bay.

He cursed and ran his hands through his hair. For one thing, the wife would see that he'd forgotten to get a haircut. For another, the prime suspect had slipped through their fingers.

Okay, the next move was, get a warrant for Blakemore as a material witness in a murder case, then go after him, get him extradited, and bring him the hell back.

But even with a warrant they'd have to find him first. How likely was that? On his home island, he'd doubtless gone to ground.

21

Monday at about half past twelve, after a chips–hamburger–soft drink lunch, Reuben was summoned for his court appearance. Johnny Cordova said, "Good luck," and Reuben walked from the cellblock into a waiting van. One of the other prisoners was the young guy with the bloody leg. None of them looked at each other. When they stopped for a red light at Carlos Rey, Reuben watched with envy a helmeted boy swerve his ten-speed past the Volvo dealership.

In the Magistrate's Court on Galisteo people were milling around, there was lots of going and coming, but as far as he could tell nothing seemed to get done. He looked around for a familiar face and saw Magda there in the back row in her floppy wide-brim hat. She waved and smiled and dabbed a handkerchief at her eyes, and he shrugged that it was nothing, he was all right.

The waits were long. Right in the middle of a hearing, somebody would approach the bench and everything would stop while the judge gave his attention to some new development. The "resident" with the bloody leg bandage went to sleep and subsided slowly onto Reuben's shoulder. Reuben kept shoving him upright, where he'd stay for about a minute.

It was almost four o'clock when his turn finally came. A court clerk told him to step up before the bench and plead Not Guilty. That was a relief. He wasn't guilty, but he wondered how the clerk knew that. Not Guilty turned out to be the only plea you could enter here, he never knew why.

The judge was genial and smiling and he asked lots of questions. How long have you been in Santa Fe, son? Not long, huh. So, have you got a job? Waiter, eh? Married? Live-in girlfriend? No family at all in the area? From New York, huh.

Reuben was pleased that the judge took an interest, but shocked when his bail was set at five hundred thousand dollars. He opened his mouth to protest, but the judge's gavel came down.

"Next!"

When he got back to the cell, Johnny Cordova laughed at him. "Man, he asked you all them questions to find out if you had any ties would bind you here, like a job or a family or a woman. Anything'd keep you from jumping bail. And you didn't give him none. So he fixed your bail so high you not likely to say farewell to this fancy hotel."

Tuesday morning he was told he had a visitor. Magda,
he thought. He was ushered down a hallway to a series
of walk-in-closet-size visiting booths. Another red door
closed behind him and he sat at a stainless steel counter
facing a glass wall.

On the other side of the glass, a tall young man
dropped down in the chair opposite with a smile that
screwed up his small features and puddled them in the
middle of his face. He had on a plaid western shirt with
pearl buttons, a cowhide vest, and green and yellow
lizard-skin western boots. He leaned forward and his
mouth formed words Reuben couldn't hear. He laughed
and reached for the phone on the wall, motioning Reuben
to do the same.

"Hi're you?" he inquired.

He was wearing a visitor's badge with his name on it:
Charley Buck Bean. Was that some kind of a joke?

Reuben asked, suspicious, "Who are you?"

"I'm your ticket outa here!" His visitor smiled con-
spiratorially and his lower eyelids curved up in the middle
and he peered out over them with eyes the shape of nail
clippings. He squirmed his shoulder up close to the glass.

22

"I'm your bail bondsman, friend. Name's Charley Buck Bean."

He screwed himself around and looked at the door behind him, then said confidentially into his phone, "Actually, Pa's the bail bondsman but he taken me in with him, see I make somethin' of myself."

"I can't make bail," Reuben said.

"Sure you can. You awreddy been arraigned, ha'n'tcha?" Again that disturbing little smile.

"Yeah," Reuben said, "but I don't have five hundred thousand on me."

Charley Buck laughed and took out a sheaf of papers. " 'At's all been taken care of. Your bail's been posted at the Sheriff's Department an' he's awreddy issued your release. Just sign these, will ya."

Smiling, face close to the glass, the bail bondsman shoved the papers through the slot. "I got a name for you right there," he said, pointing to the papers. Then hunched over he looked around again at the red door behind him and lowered his voice in the phone. "But 'at's not your real one, is it. Or maybe it is!" Rearing back, in the voice of discovery, "And they give you another one out on the Coast. Right?"

The man had to be on something. "I don't know what you're talking about."

"I'm your *bail* bondsman." As if maybe that point hadn't gotten across.

"What'd you say your name was?"

"Bean," the stranger said.

Reuben smiled sardonically. "Any kin to Judge Roy?"

Charley Buck searched his brain. "Roy-Roy," he said. "Not as I know of."

Reuben shook his head and, curious, pulled the papers

toward him. "Think I've got five hundred thousand dollars, you've gotta be nuts. I don't even know anybody's got five hundred thousand dollars."

"*Sure* you do," Charley Buck said. "Anyway, it's not five hunderd thousand! When it's cash it's only ten percent."

Reuben nodded. "Ten percent of five hundred thousand. Right. That's fifty thousand. What're you, some kind of ambulance chaser or something?" He shoved the papers back in the slot, but smiling like they were just kidding around, Charley Buck Bean shot out a hand and stopped them. He took a ballpoint pen out of his vest pocket and hit the butt rapidly with his thumb, thumping down the nib. "I marked the places need your John Henry."

Reuben said into his phone, "What *is* this? What do you want with me?"

Bean leaned close to the glass, glanced over his shoulder, and said low, "A party has paid your bail, for Crissake. Just sign the damn things." He dropped the ballpoint in the slot on top of the papers.

"Wait a minute. Are you telling me somebody paid fifty thousand dollars to get me out of here?"

"Key-rect," said Charley Buck, lounging back in his chair. He pointed to the papers and repeated, "I checked places require your signature."

Reuben scraped back his chair, stood up, and scuffed around in a circle. He stopped in front of the glass and leaned on the counter and took up the phone again. "What are these?" The papers.

"One on top's your release form," said Charley Buck.

"Release form," Reuben repeated. "I'm about to be released."

" 'At's what I been *tellin* you," Charley Buck said. " 'At's what bail *is*. 'At next one," tapping the glass, "is your Conditions of Release."

"Yeah? What's it say?"

"Hell, man, read it!" Charley Buck swiveled to look at the door behind him again, and rattled off, "Says you cannot enter any establishment known to serve alcohol— 'at means a bar—you pledge to obey all state and city ord'nances, and you may not leave the boundaries of the state of New Mexico without permission of the court as all charges are still pending against you."

"Okay, what's the catch?"

" 'At last one," Bean said, "is a copy of the charges. You got to sign 'em all."

Reuben picked up the last sheet and put it down again.

" 'At one there's your Notice to Appear form. It's a formality, man." Drumming his fingers on the counter.

"Appear where?"

Bean's eyes rolled up with exasperation. "Appear at any future *hearings*." He bent over and, not looking at Reuben, started shaking his head and rapping the stainless steel shelf with his forefingers, apparently in time to music he'd turned on in his head.

"What future hearings?"

"Well, say," still rapping, "like a preliminary hearing. Tha'd be held in District Court, though in your case there won't be one. Your case'll go straight to grand jury if they press murder charges."

"*Murder* charges!"

Now he was subtly twitching his shoulders to the imaginary rock. "Just sign, come on, sign," he said, "and we're outa here."

"Wait a minute. Let me understand this."

"Look," Bean said—he stopped rapping the counter and pointed—" 'at last there is your Release Form—you know, to get back your personal propitty, stuff they took away from you when they brought you in."

Reuben said, "There's some mistake. You've got the wrong . . ." *Fifty thousand dollars.* If what Bean said was true, then somebody badly wanted him out of here. Who? He asked warily, "Who put up the money?"

Bean leaned toward the glass, smiling like they had a secret. He pointed. "It says right there."

Reuben looked down and read aloud, "Curtis Mitchell Agency." He looked up. "What the hell's the Curtis Mitchell Agency?"

Bean ducked and smiled up at Reuben with his little slit eyes. "Come on," he said. "It's a Hollywood talent agency." He winked.

"Talent agency!"

"*You* know. Agencies that handle the stars." He glanced over his shoulder again, checking the door. "Stars, directors, people in the *industry*." Another wink.

"You got an eye tick or something?"

Bean laughed like that was a good one.

"Who are they representing *in this case*?"

Bean shook his head. "Sorry, I can't tell you that." One lick of his limp brown hair fell over his forehead and he shook it back.

"What do you mean, you can't tell me?"

"That is *the one thing* these agencies keep to theirselves. They won't tell *me*!" he said triumphantly.

"I don't get it."

"Well, look at it thisaway. Say you got this very famous client, and say this very famous client wants to buy a propitty. Maybe a life story, say, to make a TV movie or something. And say if this very famous client, who is also very rich—" another conspiratorial wink "—if this person was to let it be known *he* was the one wanting to buy this particular propitty, why, the seller would naturally hold out for a fortune. See what I mean?" He waited.

Reuben nodded. "Go on."

"Okay, so this famous person has his agency represent him in the negotiations. Thataway if the seller is anxious to sell, he—or she, of course—would be scairt to hold out for too much or the deal might fall th'oo. And the anonymous famous person gets the propitty for a lot less money. If you follow."

Reuben slumped back in the chair. He considered for a moment while Bean watched, then reached for the papers and started signing.

Bean leaned into the glass. "Ain'cha gone tell me who you are? You look a little like Tom Cruise with a permanent."

Reuben finished signing.

"Look," said Charley Buck Bean. "I hadn' got it in me to be a bail bondsman. No kiddin, 'at'd be a life sentence. When we get outa here, less go someplace and have a drink. I got some songs I wrote."

Reuben said, "I'm not supposed to go near a bar, remember."

"Yeah, but who's gonna know?"

He held onto the papers a moment longer. If somebody wanted him out of here bad enough to put up that kind of money, hadn't he better stay where he was? But then he shoved the papers back under the slot, and the bail bondsman grabbed them and folded them and stood up, stuffing them in his vest pocket.

"Okay," Reuben said, "how do I get out of here?"

Strumming a few chords on an imaginary guitar, Charley Buck spun around in a circle with his eyes closed, then stopped and leaned over the stainless steel shelf. "You could show 'em to somebody," he said. "Like maybe 'at agency. I got a lotta talent. Ever'body says so."

23

As soon as he'd got rid of Charley Buck Bean—it wasn't easy—he hitchhiked, then walked the rest of the way home, hugged Magda, and had the luxury of a long hot shower.

When he headed across the compound to the rig, Magda called out her kitchen window, "Where are you going? I've put on a pot of chili!"

"Tesuque!" he yelled back. "To find out who's messing with my life."

"No, hang on! Wait a minute!"

He waited. She came out on her back stoop with the Sunday *New Mexican*. "Here, look at this."

He read and cursed. They'd left for Jamaica, the whole bunch. The paper salivated over details of their Santa Fe stay, treating the murder of an old lady as little more than a scenario.

He rolled up the paper and slapped his leg with it. Now what?

He still had one more errand. The business of the bail nagging at him, he got in the rig and headed out to Perdita Waldheimer's to return the Caddy keys. He found himself consulting the rearview mirror as he drove. A small white car followed at a distance behind him. He slowed and the white car slowed. He sped up and the white car sped up.

It had occurred to him that he'd been set free because somebody wanted him available. For what? People were playing with his life.

He slowed and drove past the Waldheimer mailbox, and the white car slowed behind him. He pulled off on the shoulder. The white car sped up and pulled around in front of him and stopped. Reuben got out and walked up to the car window. Charley Buck Bean turned up at him that slice of a smile.

Reuben said, "What the hell do you think you're doing?"

"All I wanna know—just tell me—who *are* you?"

Reuben opened the white car's door and hauled Charley Buck out by his western shirt.

"Hey!"

Reuben said, "I'll tell you who I am. I'm Clint Eastwood and you're making me mad."

Charley Buck grinned. "Aw, you ain't Clint Eastwood. You ain't old enough."

"Junior," Reuben said.

But Charley Buck was suspicious. "You puttin' me on?"

"You want to find out," Reuben said, "catch the next plane to LAX. Go see the agency. Tell them I sent you."

Charley Buck sagged back in confusion against the white car.

"Take it or leave it," Reuben said, turning to the rig.

Charley Buck called after him, "Maybe you ought to gimme a note or something."

Charley Buck ran up with a bail bond form.

Reuben turned it over and scrawled on the back "Clint Eastwood, Jr." "Here you go. That ought to do it."

He did a U-turn and left Charley Buck staring after him.

24

Perdita had been dozing. She often caught little cat-naps during the day. She found it refreshing, especially since she'd been wakened in the middle of the night. Old age was an annoyance. It was a blessing nobody told the young about the end of the journey. It might discourage them from setting out.

Sometimes she scolded herself for being such a hermit, but, truly, she did not much like company. Social chitchat, so false and meaningless, bored her stiff now she was older. Older. She smiled at the word. You were never *old*, just *older*. *Older* people. *Older* women. When you are *older*. Well, she had decided to be frankly *old*. There were advantages. You could be crotchety, say what you think, do as you pleased without having to please anybody. And none of her old friends were left. The best people were all dead. She and Jack made do without much conversation, and he was the one managed the women in the kitchen. She only needed one of them, but how now could she let the other one go? Oh well, it was a big house, and though these days she hardly saw a third of it from one month to the next, she supposed it had to be kept up.

Appearances, appearances. She sighed and dozed with her chin on her chest.

"A visitor, mum."

She jerked awake. Jack, nose in the air, had ushered in a young man in jeans. But it seemed he only wanted to return the Caddy keys. She hadn't known they were missing. Wasn't he the one drove Charlotte and Simon to Tesuque?

"Sit down, sit down, young man. Jack, some Irish coffee, if you please."

Reuben hesitated. He'd made up his mind what his next move would be, and he'd better get on with it. But he dropped down on the hearth where a small fire burned. She wanted him to tell her all he knew about the murder.

It turned out he didn't know as much as she did. Then mellowed by the Irish coffee he felt the urge to explain himself.

She listened with her eyes on him.

"So what I'm going to do," he finished, "I'm going to find out who framed me then bailed me out, and why. I intend to know what the hell—excuse me—is going on. I'm going after them. I mean to clear my name."

Perdita heard him out and shook her head. "If you leave here, won't you be skipping bail? I mean, if they catch you, couldn't they get you for contempt of court?"

He hadn't thought of that. He saw the shrewdness in the blue eyes behind the little pinch-on glasses. "What would they do to me?"

"I believe they would put you back in jail and keep you there until your trial comes up. That could be months."

He thought of the Detention Center and shook his head. "I'm not going back."

She nodded. "I see. Yes. You're flying off to a strange place, a large island you've never seen before, with high-lands and forests and large tracks of mountain land, where some are unfriendly to strangers and you know nobody. And you're going to flush out a murderer who may be dangerous. That's a little like Nemo chasing a car—if you catch him, what'll you do with him?"

Stubborn, he looked away. She thought he was nuts.

"All this, of course, assuming you make it undetected out of the country," she added. "And assuming you have a passport."

He'd never thought of a passport.

She asked gently, "Perhaps you have a birth certificate?"

He did. But where had he put the damn thing?

"Your birth certificate will do," she said. "Along with your driver's license, it will get you into the country. Have you any money?"

She opened the drawer in the little round table beside her chair and put in his hand a bulky white legal-size envelope labeled in a large, looping hand: HOUSEHOLD EXPENSES. "Here, take it, take it."

"What is it?"

But it was clear what it was. Inside was a sheaf of hundred-dollar bills.

He tried to give it back, but she said with a dismissive flap of her hand, "No-no, keep it. I want you to do some-thing for me."

25

Jane Boll was still laid up with her hip, so she sent Matilde from the plantation into Turtle Bay to see to the condominium overlooking the beach. It belonged to Dame Charlotte but was only used when guests overflowed the house and had to be billeted in town.

Charlotte had bought it sight-unseen some years earlier due to just such a necessity. The decor was still that of the former tenants, an East Indian family from Tobago, and ornate with Turkish rugs and peacock chairs and urns full of ostrich feathers. Charlotte had left it as it was because it amused her.

The condominium had been empty for months, but now, since the news had come of Charlotte's death, Jane Boll, tall and spare, housekeeper and tyrant, had ordered the grumbling Matilde to bring the penthouse up to Jane Boll's demanding standards. With a funeral in the offing guests would be arriving.

With a frosty Coca-Cola in hand and her bare feet propped up on the railing, Matilde was lounging out on the condo balcony overlooking the bay, as still today as a housecat's saucer. No breeze stirred the tops of the palms below. She had the air-conditioning going full blast inside, and she'd left the sliding doors open to get the benefit of it.

She had decided to make it a long day, maybe have lunch at the Lobster Pot, where her friend Julie was waitress. Matilde particularly liked the Lobster Pot's rice-and-bean dish, and the blackened fish. Also, since the condominium had a number of bathing suits and robes left behind by guests, she thought she might go down to the beach and flirt with the muscle men hawking trips to the reef in their glass-bottom boats. She had no intention of going in the water. She was deathly afraid of it. She couldn't swim. But she thought her figure was best set off by a bikini.

A giant cruise ship had berthed the night before on one point of the bay. The restaurants in town would be crowded. But not the Lobster Pot. The Lobster Pot had no tables set out under trees, no richly foliaged hillside with waterfalls tumbling into pools of colored fish. It was known mostly to the locals, but it had the best Island food in town.

She was thinking she might top off lunch with an ice cream cone from the shop up the street when behind her she heard the key turn in the lock. Then the dead bolt shot back in its slot. She smiled, expecting the maintenance man who'd eyed her in the elevator. Doubtless he'd decided to fix a nonexistent drip in the plumbing.

She arranged her face into a pretty look of surprise, but turning discovered it wasn't the maintenance man at all.

26

It was the tail end of the hurricane season and Caribbean resorts were a bargain. Flights were overbooked with people willing to gamble that the storms were over. Reuben got as far as DFW, then camped out at the airport waiting for a standby to Miami. Whenever he sighted a security uniform, paranoid he ducked into a rest room. But finally, after sleeping most of the night with his head on his athletic bag, he flew on to Miami. He spent the short flight to Montego Bay looking down on mackerel clouds diluting the blue of the Gulf, chewing over the hazards Perdita had mentioned. He had a habit of taking on more than he could handle.

At Sangster International, Armisted Whatley unwound his lanky frame from a chair in the gate area and came forward. They shook hands. Reuben thanked Whatley for meeting him.

"Oh, my pleasure, my pleasure," the historian said in his high breaking voice.

Reuben smiled. In return for this meeting, Perdita Waldheimer had pledged a substantial gift to the historical society in memory of Dame Charlotte. He was struck again by the man's appearance. The contrast of

black skin with the silver skullcap of hair made his face
an ebony carving.

The historian sped through Montego Bay traffic,
weaving, jumping lanes, and glancing at Reuben as he
spoke. Reuben fastened his seat belt.

"As you'd suspect, I enjoy delving into the island's
past," Whatley said. "I have engaged the help of a
friend with similar interests, a newspaperman . . . This is
Gloucester Avenue . . ." But Reuben didn't take his eyes
off the road. "And of course the Kingston police, who
have made their files available to me for research on
more than one occasion."

The small white Toyota swerved into a hotel drive,
dipped abruptly to the curb, and stopped. Reuben lurched
forward, caught by the seat belt.

"Shall we sit on the terrace?"

He followed Whatley across a tiled lobby. Mirror
walls, tanks of fish, a large gilt standing cage with a big
white bird that called after them in a voice that sounded
electronic, "Hi guys! Pretty pol!" Its crest shot up in a
startling fan.

The terrace overlooked the beach. They sat in webbed
chairs at a round table under a flowered umbrella. It was
early. Most of the people at the other tables seemed to be
locals.

Whatley ordered Blue Mountain coffee. Reuben, who
had breakfasted on low-fat pretzels on the plane, ordered
chowder, a club sandwich, a glass of milk, and got imme-
diately to the point. "Is it true that Blakemore's the heir?"

"From all I have been able to discover," Whatley said.
"Dame Charlotte, as you know, had no *chil*dren. She met
Saxe-Ogilvy during the war. I believe after the invasion
of Normandy she nursed him in a *field* hospital.

"Thank you," he said to the waiter bringing his coffee. "Saxe-Ogilvy was a colonel in a British armored division. It was his second marriage. His first was a hasty affair following a brief furlough romance. It broke up during his long overseas assignment in Africa."

"No children of that marriage either?"

"None that we know of." He tapped his fingertips together close to his chest and gazed out upon the bay where an armada of sailboats lay at anchor. "Of course, if there was a child of one of his extramarital liaisons that he then ac*know*ledged, that child would auto*ma*tically inherit."

Reuben waited for more, but apparently the man liked to create small dramas.

"Was there such a child?"

"Years ago there was talk. And from time immemorial, gossip concerning the very rich or the very famous gets disseminated in whispers—and luckily for our purposes, in print." A long manicured finger slid a clipping across the table.

Reuben scanned it and shrugged. "Any idea who she was?"

Whatley shook his head. "Alas, no. It was so long ago." Still he avoided Reuben's eyes and looked out over the bay as if making up his mind to something.

Again Reuben waited.

"There was a *sail*ing accident," Whatley said finally, "more widely reported than would be thought usual. It is all here." He retrieved his briefcase from beside his chair and fished out a sheaf of photocopies. "It happened, according to the clippings, some fifteen years following the Saxe-Ogilvy couple's return to the island after the war. The lost sailboat, as you will see *here*—" he selected several of the clippings and passed them to Reuben "—was called a Honeymoon Sloop. They were beautiful wooden boats—Norwegian, I believe—and built for heavy northern seas. They were not *large*, but they had deep, heavy keels weighing around four *thou*sand pounds. You'd expect that kind of boat to be safe in these waters."

Reuben scanned the clippings. The sloop left port on a clear day bound for Cuba, ninety miles away. "A squall?"

"Yes, the kind you'd think this boat would *ea*sily ride out. But it never reached its desti-*neh*-tion."

Reuben scanned the articles. According to the newspapers a search turned up nothing, no debris, no life jackets. All aboard were given up for lost.

"Who was on board?" he asked.

"The boat belonged to a friend of Saxe-Ogilvy's. The newspapers—" he tapped the clippings "—indicate as you will *see* that the man sailed alone, but gossip columns, as you will also see, just there," leaning over and putting a long, elegant finger to another of the clippings, "hinted there was also a young woman. Apparently Saxe-Ogilvy, almost sixty at the time, liked his mistresses to be little more than *chil*dren."

"The friend was eloping with Saxe-Ogilvy's *mistress*?"

It seemed to him Whatley had waited for that. Another little drama. "Or perhaps the friend was re*mov*ing her from the island to avoid a scandal."

"You think they survived?"

Whatley studied his hands clasped in front of him on the table. His eyebrows rose. "Perhaps," he said. "Or perhaps the friend relieved Saxe-Ogilvy *per*manently of this difficulty."

Reuben fell back in his chair and looked at the historian. "You mean he threw her overboard."

Armisted Whatley shrugged. "If they caused trouble, black mistresses of white landowners sometimes suffered *expeditious* fates."

Reuben said, "So without any evidence you've maybe got an old unsolved killing, but I don't see how it's relevant to the Tesuque murder."

Whatley looked noncommittally at the bay. "Only," he said, "if the girl were *preg*nant at the time and if she survived."

After a moment Reuben whistled softly. "You're saying there could be another heir."

Whatley nodded. "Perhaps, if Saxe-Ogilvy acknowledged the child."

"Why would he, if he meant to have the woman killed?"

Whatley lifted his hands and dropped them heavily on the chair arms.

"Nice guy, this Saxe-Ogilvy."

"I see you are getting the *pic*ture."

"Is any of this true?"

Whatley shrugged.

Reuben glanced at the dates on the clippings. "It all happened forty-some-odd years ago."

Whatley was watching him. "At the beginning of the hurricane season," he said. "The time of storms."

Reuben tried to judge the ages of the people at Tesuque that day but gave it up. "Any more information about the Barbon case?"

With a sigh, Whatley produced another folder and handed it over. Reuben perused its contents at length. Twenty-eight years ago, on her way home from school, a twelve-year-old girl was waylaid along a wooded path crossing a corner of Turtle Bay Plantation and raped repeatedly by a gang of local boys. The stories never mentioned race. There were no pictures of either the girl or her attackers. The boys were apprehended and charged with the crime, but the article reported no names.

"It was the policy of the police in cases involving sex crimes to withhold the names of juvenile criminals and their victims," Whatley said.

The crime had been particularly brutal—the girl had been hospitalized for some time.

"How do you know the girl was Margarite Barbon?"

"Apparently it was common knowledge." Whatley was looking past him at the bay. Reuben thought he was withholding something.

"What happened to the boys?"

"From what I've been able to determine, they each spent a couple of years in juvenile detention."

Reuben reread the newspaper stories. One boy was said to be from Turtle Bay Plantation, the others from the town.

Whatley said, "The boys would now be men in their forties."

"A woman could hold onto rage for a long time over something like that."

"But revenge upon the plantation owner? Why?" The historian shrugged. "An old lady? What could she have to do with it?"

Reuben said, "She was murdered in Margarite Barbon's bedroom."

But Whatley remained silent and the observation led no further. The waiter refilled their cups and took Reuben's chowder bowl away. He attacked the sandwich. "What do you know about Simon Blakemore?"

"We know a great deal about that young man," Whatley said with what sounded like scorn. He bent again to his briefcase.

The clippings he laid before Reuben either concerned Blakemore's leaving for Oxford University, with mention of Dame Charlotte, his benefactor, or his return to Jamaica six years later. Why six years? The article answered his question: Blakemore had also studied at the London School of Economics. And there was mention of still another part of his history that Reuben hadn't heard before. Upon his return, Simon Blakemore had spent some time at the University of the West Indies in Kingston. He turned the clipping over and saw news of rioting in Kingston at the time.

"What about Blakemore's childhood? Has he got a family?"

"His mother lives on the plantation," Whatley said.

"Still?"

Whatley sipped his coffee. "I believe so. I heard that at one time she was a house servant."

"Any siblings?"

"Several sisters, all older and, I believe, married and dispersed here and there around the island." He hesitated. "And one brother."

The hesitation wasn't lost on Reuben. "A brother?"

Whatley nodded. "Yes. Gabriel. In trouble from time to time. Keeps mostly to himself, but he can be a rabble-rouser. He's a very angry young man."

"Who's he mad at?"

The historian's hands lifted and dropped back to his chair arms. "Oh, I guess the usual—authorities, whites, whoever he perceives as having power." He shrugged. "It's a long historic holdover from Spanish times and the

British colonial system. He sees himself as a descendant of sleh-ves, as most island blacks undoubtedly are." The historian chuckled ironically. "More surely even than money or name, hatred is passed down father to son. And of course there's the other thing."

He sighed. Reuben waited.

"You know how it is—one brother black and deformed, the other light-skinned and handsome and favored by a rich patron. There lies room for enmity."

It sounded like a garbled mess. Reuben slumped back in his chair and looked up at the umbrella's ruffle stirring in a breeze that brought with it the smell of flowers. "What about Señor Ribera?"

Whatley said in an icy voice devoid of the usual note of amusement, "As far as I know, the man has never before set foot on the island. He is only here because his way was paid and his meals and lodging provided—and perhaps he hopes the visit will lend authenticity to his outrageous lectures on Caribbean history." Armisted Whatley was turning his match folder in his fingers and irritably tapping it on the table. "But I know for a fact that Ribera is a pauper. The man latches onto wealthy wherever he can."

The historian clearly hated the little Spaniard.

"You said Branwell Kane had some connection here."

Whatley's face relaxed. He smiled. "I have heard it said that one of his many *alliances* was with a Caribbean woman from Los Angeles."

Reuben laughed. "And one was Chinese, one East Indian, and another from Samoa."

Whatley chuckled. "Apparently the man likes women trained to subservience by their cultures."

"Do you know the woman's name?"

Whatley shook his head. "I don't even know that she exists."

"What about the scriptwriter?"

"Reybuhr?"

Reuben nodded. "When he was in Tesuque he mentioned vacationing here."

"A fact of which I was already aware," Whatley said coldly.

Reuben watched the historian frown and consider his next words.

"I believe he is what's known in the States as a 'dinge queen.' " The historian spat out the phrase.

Reuben said, "You mean he likes black men."

"And some say boys."

"And that's what he was doing in Jamaica?"

"I assume so."

"What about Datrey Moss?" Whatley's affection for the young novelist had been obvious in Tesuque.

The match folder was suddenly stilled. "Yes? What about him?"

"Was he a friend of Simon Blakemore's? They're about the same age. Maybe they went to school together."

Whatley said in a voice that was tightly controlled, "They knew each other as boys. I wouldn't say they are friends."

Reuben nodded, expecting no more on the subject of Datrey Moss, but Whatley continued. "That young man never had the opportunities of a Simon Blakemore. He had no *background*, no rich patron, no scholarship because as a youngster he had to fight dyslexia. Nobody made *his* way easy. But the boy can *write*, and your American publishers are enamored just now with—ethnics, as they call us—so he'll be all right. Better than all right. Jamaica is proud of that young man."

Reuben was nodding, listening not so much to the words as to the music. Watching the historian's reaction, he kept his voice casual. "Do you think he ever met Nat Reybuhr before, perhaps here in Jamaica?"

Armisted Whatley drew himself up. "Absolutely not!"

Reuben looked out to the beach where a squatting boy put sand in a red bucket with a yellow shovel and a couple strolled hand-in-hand. The bringing together of these people had to be purposeful, or else a huge coincidence. He didn't believe in coincidence.

Back on the sidewalk under the hotel's barrel awning, Whatley handed Reuben the keys to the Toyota. "Be my guest, as you Americans say."

Surprised, and grateful once again to Perdita Waldheimer, Reuben watched a cab pull alongside the curb and Whatley fold himself in.

"Be careful, young man." The historian waved as the cab pulled away.

Reuben turned on the Toyota's air-conditioning—it was hot in Jamaica. The rental car came with a tourist brochure commanding him to DRINK OUR RUM, DANCE REGGAE, CHARTER A YACHT, PLAY GOLF, WINDSURF THE NORTH COAST, CLIMB THE WATERFALL. Fat chance, he thought. The car also supplied him with a map of the island.

He propped the map on the steering wheel. Once he'd got his directions straight he pulled out into traffic, spun the wheel wildly to avoid a head-on collision, got back on the left side of the road, and told himself *Stay there.* He headed for Jamaica's north coast and Turtle Bay, passing the spot where the map said they'd filmed the coastal scenes in *Doctor No*. It also boasted that Ian Fleming, who wrote the James Bond series, had once lived on the island.

A little farther and he drove past the bay where Columbus had anchored his crippled ship and lay stranded for months. And still farther, the red-dusted harbor where they loaded bauxite from the mines and a rusty-looking freighter lay at anchor.

Then he was passing the famous waterfall plunging down through tropical foliage. The brochure said you could rent rubber shoes and climb it from the beach to the park above. Apparently plenty of people opted to try. Water cascaded over chains of them holding hands and squealing and struggling to keep their footing up the slippery stone steps of the falls.

A little farther on his map told him to turn left. He followed its advice and looped into town.

He found Turtle Towers easily and parked the Toyota in a lot littered with the large squashed pods of blooming trees. Once out of the car's air-conditioning, he began to sweat. It felt good. It was hard to work up a sweat in high dry Santa Fe. He locked his bag in the trunk and, following Perdita's instructions, presented himself to the condominium management as a guest of Turtle Bay Plantation. They politely requested him to wait while they telephoned up to the house.

27

When Jane Boll frowned, the lines of her face converged in the middle like tracks coming into a station. But once she'd hung up the telephone she left off her annoyance and limped with her cane to the verandah wrapping the plantation house like the deck of a ship. For though she frowned and scolded and commanded the men to keep a sharp eye on things, in spite of herself she was fascinated by the filming.

Haphazardly shoved against the wall or ranged along the railings were enough round-back wicker chairs with floor-length skirts to accommodate a resort hotel. She had pulled a wicker chaise close to the railing so that, laying her cane aside and keeping a stern face for anyone who chose to look in through the vines, she could enjoy the entertainment.

Ever since they arrived, the film people were all over the place, flying here and there like there was no tomorrow. Several had paid their respects, those she supposed were in charge. After that, she had hardly spoken to them except for the big fat one who took the time yesterday to sit with her on the verandah dressed to the nines in a big curly wig and knee pants with buckles, sweating streams that threatened to spoil his makeup. She chuckled when she saw him in that ridiculous costume. She would not admit even to herself that she liked him.

When he teased and flirted with her as if she were a girl, and asked her advice, and wanted to hear her life story, she was at pains to retain her dignity as suzerain here.

The macaw, still out there on his chosen perch, was a big colorful blossom in the foliage. She worried about the bird. First, he'd left off his bad-tempered ways and set up a pitiful crying, calling as he hadn't in years, swooping high and low till he settled on that particular limb of the nutmeg tree and stayed there. Eerie, such carrying on. She knew it was because the bird had learned in his own uncanny way that Charlotte was dead. Ravens, too, had that power.

Sitting there bolt upright on her chaise with her leg stretched out in front of her, and screened by the bougain-villea and the creamy white frangipani, while the woman director's voice came over the bullhorn she reflected upon the will of the Lord and the shortness of life, though heaven knows Charlotte had been no spring chicken. Jane Boll had scolded her enough about running off that way. And that foolhardy wedding! Charlotte was already old when the boy was running around here barefoot in short pants, a pretty little thing.

In the years they'd been together, Jane Boll had moved steadily up from maid to housekeeper to friend and confi-dante. Now at her own advanced age, life did seem sur-prisingly short whereas always before there had been time enough to do whatever you had to do. But she told herself the girl—as she still thought of Charlotte when-ever she defied the dictates of good sense—the girl had challenged the Lord, running off like that, and the Lord was not to be dared.

So now it was over, her long association with Char-lotte, who even as a young woman had been difficult, arriving here still in her uniform, a little redheaded thing with the macaw on her shoulder. Spirited, too, a match for the widower set in his wicked ways and much older than his bride. But a fine-looking man, Jane Boll grudgingly acknowledged, trim and tall with that military way of carrying himself.

It had not been an easy match. He had struck Charlotte once and dared her to interfere with his life, and she had banished him from the bedroom with a pistol under her pillow. That went on for quite a while. She'd forgotten now what that was all about, though she'd known at the time because Charlotte kept nothing from her. Maybe some to-do about a fufu woman. The marriage never recovered. Charlotte had reinstated him for the sole purpose of making a child, though sadly that never happened.

She supposed Charlotte's minions, the good gray doctor and the old plump judge, were making the necessary arrangements. So far, she'd had no details from them, only the terrible news that Charlotte was dead. Well, hers not to wonder why. In time they would let her know whatever she needed to know. Meanwhile, the house was ready.

She sat bolt upright with her lame leg resting before her, jealously watching should the film people destroy one iota of the property—trees, lawns, flowers. The clatter out there had quieted. They were getting ready. One of the men poked at the macaw with a bamboo pole, trying to move him from the nutmeg tree. But the macaw's white cheeks went slowly red, a bad sign, and he snapped at the pole with his hooked beak. The woman director called, "It's all right! Leave him!" and they stopped tormenting the bird and left him where he was.

He had been a continual nuisance to the filmmakers, flying at first one then another. But now he'd lost his spirit. His wings hung loose from his body, and his head lolled off his neck as if he were dozing. Poor bird, he was another one getting old.

No telling what it would be this afternoon. This morning the slave uprising took place before her unbelieving eyes, the cuffies attacking everything in sight, screaming bloody murder. And when that was over, swarming over the place like rudeboys, giving her a turn.

This afternoon would be something else. In this business of making movies time was out of joint. In the morning everything gone to the devil, dead bodies heaped up or lying bloody on the grass, but this afternoon it was all smiles and bowing and "yessah, massah," the dandified young owner bringing his bride home from across the sea, and those same local extras, all gussied up in wigs and knee pants, lining the path from the old-timey horse carriage (now where did they find that thing?) to the verandah steps where the house servants waited and she'd had to move farther off behind the bougainvillea.

There on the chaise, she remembered the day the real master brought Charlotte home, a young nurse already knighted for valor on the field of battle. Though Jane Boll had vowed to herself she would not, once again she gave in to grief. She hoped someone had been with her old friend at the end, and she prayed sweet Jesus she herself would not pass alone.

Then she put morbid thoughts aside and thanked the Lord she'd had the foresight to send that worthless Matilde to ready the place in town now that funeral guests had begun arriving, for she assumed that's what the phone call from the condominium management had signified.

And where was that Matilde anyway? She should have returned by now. It didn't do to let the girl out of sight for a minute.

28

Reuben took the elevator to the tenth floor and let himself in. He dropped his athletic bag in one of the peacock chairs and tossed his windbreaker on a tapestry couch covered with big colored birds.

His image moving in the mirror wall startled him. He was jumpy. He looked out the sliding doors to the balcony and admired the view of the bay. In the kitchen he spotted a beer can in the trash and upended it over the sink. A few drops trickled out. He was surprised. But his shirt clung to his back and his hair curled wetly on his neck, so maybe in this humid climate a few drops could survive in a can for days. He found another beer in the refrigerator and was grateful.

He explored. One hall, off the entry, led to a couple of bedrooms, and a bath at the end of the corridor. Another, off the living room, went to the master suite. Great, he'd take that one for himself.

But he stopped in the doorway. A pair of chinos and a white shirt lay carelessly tossed on the queen-size bed. And dropped on top of a pair of tassel loafers on the floor, a pair of dark silk socks holding the shape of somebody's feet. Then he saw a man's kit open on the toilet tank in the adjoining bath.

The place was occupied.

Shoved partly under the bed was one of those pull-bags on little wheels that people drag through airports. He swung it onto the bed and opened it.

A place for everything and everything in its place. Black leather bedroom slippers still in their slots. A soiled white shirt with crumbs of pine needles in the pocket. A navy silk suit and red vest he thought he recognized.

So where was Blakemore? He must have changed out of the rumpled suit and dirty shirt when he came out of the mountains, and then flown to Jamaica in the shirt and chinos on the bed.

Okay, but something begged for his attention. It was those tassel loafers. Blakemore had changed, but into what? The slippers were still in the bag, and the bag still packed. Was the man wandering around barefoot and naked?

He searched the condominium and found in one of the closets a collection of bathing suits, women's on hangers and, above them on the shelf, men's trunks. And on the floor a jumbled pile of flip-flops.

It was the flip-flops that made the connection: Blakemore had gone for a swim.

He was indebted to Perdita Waldheimer. He wanted to do what she'd asked of him, which was to *find Simon*, but he couldn't help thinking: What if the man is dangerous?

29

Matilde was bent over peering through the square of exposed glass in the bottom of the boat. Eugene dangled his legs over the side of the pirate ship, watching.

"I can't see a thing!" she squealed. "Oooh, there they go!" Being cute. Showing off for him.

"You enjoyin the pretty fishes, dahlin?"

Matilde ignored him, pouting, peering through the square of glass into the pellucid water.

"Be glad to take you out the reef, dahlin. You want to see fishes, that's where they mek they homes."

"Not for a million bucks," she said. Not looking up at him, playing with the rope that tethered the boat to the pirate ship. "Think I let you dunk me with a mask on my face, you crehzie, bwai."

In that little string thing spattered with big colored flowers, she chattered away like a bright-colored bird.

"You ain live till you see them reef fishes," he said. "Red. Yella. Blue. You name it."

"I *tole* you, I am afreh-d of the water. I cyain swim, I drown if I go out there and the little fishes would eat me!"

"I hole onto you, dahlin. I won't let go."

The sun sank behind a bank of clouds rolling up over the horizon. She said, "Oooh, Lord, don't let it storm."

Eugene laughed. "What you think, he lis'nin to you? He busy up there checkin off his clipboard and you kotch his attention, he say to the angel, 'Whoa, hole up on at storm down there'?"

A Jet Ski zoomed by, kicking up a wake that rocked the glass-bottom boat. Matilde sank onto the bench that circled the gunnels. "I'moan th'ow up he does that again." Fist in her eyes, crocodile tears. "How come you bring me out here an treat me this way? Let me come on board."

"In a little, hon. You enjoyin yourse'f, you know you are."

A can of Red Strike beer appeared in a hand over Eugene's shoulder, and as he popped the tab the Jet Ski rocked the little boat again and Matilde fluttered up and subsided with cute little cries. She was something else. Eugene would like a little of that. He liked his women daffy. You could play with them.

A voice behind him said, "Damn!"

Eugene said, "What the matter?"

"Nothin. I don't know. Hand me them glasses."

"Come on, mahn, reach behind you. They hangin on the mast."

30

A beach boy snapped open a chaise and, hot and tired, Reuben dropped into it. In flip-flops and trunks from the condo, he'd walked the sand crescent from one end to the other, but no sign of Simon Blakemore. He wasn't disappointed. He hadn't exactly kept his word to Perdita. But for a while he could put that aside.

He watched a boy out in the bay speed around in a sleek black thing like a cross between a beetle and a snowmobile, the boy kneeling or standing up, bending to steer, reeling in tight circles, kicking up a wake.

The water looked cool and inviting. He dropped the towel he'd brought from the condo, and walked to the water's edge and tried the temperature with his toes. Then he splashed out to where the sea floor dropped, sucked in his breath, and dived. He swam out to the rope and hung on, rocked by the Jet Ski's wake.

Farther out, an old sailing vessel wallowed heavily in the bay. Probably a fake, he thought, for the tourists. He let go, ducked under the rope, and swam farther out with the crawl he'd learned at the 14th Street Y and improved at the Fort Marcy compound in Santa Fe. Breathe, face under, stroke, breathe. The water was cooler out here. Breathe, reach, stroke.

He'd passed the pirate ship and was ready to turn back when—face in the water—something grabbed him around the legs. Panicked, he thought sharks! He kicked, trying to free himself and get his head above water. But his legs were held in a tightening vise. And in plain sight of people on the beach, he swallowed half the Caribbean as whatever it was pulled him toward the bottom of the bay.

31

The slave girl Esme had just been purchased by the overseer and brought to the plantation. The scene was the plantation owner's first attempt to seduce her. Margarite Barbon had been tempted to put it off till they were further into the shooting, but this was the scene that would set the relationship in Zoe McNaire's viscera and make the rest of the film work. They'd done several runthroughs, pacing it, moving the cameras around. Brian Tanaka, the cinematographer, whom Margarite Barbon greatly respected for the uncanny quality of light he managed to capture, had urged her to put aside her impatience and wait for the sun to drop, letting the shadows fall in a certain way, and she had bowed to his judgment.

She'd gone over the scene again and again with Zoe McNaire, who, she thought, smiled pleasantly, not looking at her, thinking her own thoughts and only pretending to pay attention, though now and then the girl would look up and meet the director's eye with a little infuriating smile, as if they shared some unspoken secret. The director had a constant fight with herself about this girl. It made the filming harder than it otherwise would have been.

She had watched Zoe rehearse the scene with Branwell Kane, and seen the starlet listen petulantly but attentively, though to the director everything Kane said in his soft nasal voice struck her as innocuous, no more than she'd told the girl herself.

"Now, kitten, what happens here is dramatic enough without histrionics. It'll work better with a kind of—ah— tight calm, the calm before the storm, see what I mean?"

The director saw what he meant all right. It was not exactly as she had envisioned it, but she preferred waiting to see how it worked rather than dealing with the girl again.

It was these two who would make or break the film. She had realized all along that the young actor playing the slave hero was lightweight compared to Kane. All he contributed was muscles and looks. The gluttonous plantation owner had to project a voracious evil. The young hero was not really in contention. She had wanted Denzel Washington, but he was committed to other projects.

Cameras going, Margarite Barbon watched anxiously as the tension built between the two out on the lawn in front of the plantation house, Branwell Kane projecting evil with such force it apparently struck the whole watching crew.

While he tracked his prey, his words in that light nasal voice carried. "Don't forget, missy, I own you as I own my horse. I can do anything with you I like. I could chop you up as fish bait if I took a notion."

"Do," the slave girl said. "Death comes quickly. Not even time to close your eyes."

"You delicious little animal. I'll cook you with an apple in your mouth."

"Damn him! He's thrown out the script!" She was ready to yell "Cut!" but out on the lawn the slave girl said with a taunting smile, "Do, m'lord, and you'll choke on my gravy."

Margarite Barbon gasped. That wasn't in the script either. The girl was matching him line for line.

Then Kane lunged, Esme screamed, and Jane Boll woke with a start and thought she had leapt to the edge of the verandah shouting, "Get him! Get him off the girl!" If nobody else did, she'd do it herself.

But it was Charlotte could bring down a bird out of the sky. She thought she saw it now, young Charlotte flying toward the house with the reins in one hand and a brace of pheasants in the other, skidding to a stop in front of the verandah, holding up the birds for Jane to see. The girl was a regular cowboy on that white horse Ahab, who lived to be twenty-seven years old and as lame as Jane herself, grazing that very lawn where the fat man wrestled the pretty girl to the ground while she pummeled him with her little fists.

"Get him off her!" Jane Boll yelled, rising up, waving her stick. "Somebody help that young-un!"

But they all just stood around watching. Too late she realized it was make-believe. She'd made a fool of herself. It was this business of getting old that confused her.

Then that big fool Gabriel—he'd been coming every day to ask were the newlyweds back—rounded the corner of the house running, and with a cry as thrilling as Sasabonsam's caught the fat man from behind, flung him to the ground, and grabbed up the slave girl.

"Get away. Get out of here!" Jane Boll cried. "Get back to your Cockpits, you ugly thing!"

Tony Quayle hissed "Cut!" and the cinematographer was looking at her, but Margarite Barbon motioned frantically to keep the cameras rolling as Gabriel threw Zoe across his shoulder and, hunched like a black Quasimodo, fled across the lawn and plunged into the tangled vines and disappeared in the forest with his prize.

32

Reuben came to facedown on a plank floor with seawater gushing out of his mouth. He tried to rise but somebody was sitting on him. He focused on a foot close to his face, brown with a pink sole. Then pressure on his lungs again, and he gagged and threw up. A curse, and the foot yanked away. His stomach muscles went out of control trying to bring up more. Then exhausted he lay quiet. Where am I? But he wasn't sure he'd said it. A gentle rocking and he realized he was on a boat. He tried to see, and discovered he had only one good eye. The other one was swollen shut, and his hands were tied behind his back.

"Yoo-hoo!" A female voice.

"What'll you do with her?" Almost a whisper.

"Don't ask me. You the one brought her here." And louder, "You all right, dahlin?"

"I want to come on board." Little-girl whiney.

"We having a conference, dahlin. We be th'oo directly."

Off a little way, attached by a line, Reuben saw with his good eye one of the glass-bottom boats and a pretty girl dangling her feet off the bow, splashing them in the water. She looked sideways up, flirting. Bright-eyed. Dimples.

He lifted his head to shake it, but the foot mashed his cheek to the deck again. "What you doing in Turtle Bay, mahn?"

Reuben tried to twist around, see the speaker, but the foot pushed his face to the deck.

"Yoo-hoo! Euge-ene," singing it, "I'm getting thirsty!" Reuben squinted. Everything wavy, then settling. Big brown eyes, pert little nose, string bikini. And Eugene turned out to be a light-skinned man with a gap between his front teeth.

"Here, kotch!" A can of Pepsi sailed through the air. She put up her hands like shooing it away, didn't come close to catching it. The Pepsi splashed into the bay. She squealed and leaned over the side of the boat, her little ass pointing up. "Oooh. It's gone bye-bye."

"Here, honey. Don't try an kotch it this time. Just let it lan'."

The second can hit the deck of the glass-bottom boat and rolled. She scrambled around and came up with it, holding it up, letting them see.

"At's great, dahlin! You done good!"

She shook the can, aimed it at the one called Eugene, and, laughing, pulled the tab. Eugene ducked out of the Pepsi spray. "You gone lose it all, girl!"

Out of his good eye Reuben watched the Pepsi shower with a terrible sense of loss. He groaned and dropped his cheek to the deck. He may have just swallowed half the bay but he was very thirsty.

"Looka there," a low voice said, "mahn's thirsty."

Back into his line of vision came a smiling Eugene, who produced from somewhere a clear plastic glass and poured.

"This what you want, mahn? Here, lemme hep you."

He took hold of a fistful of Reuben's hair and pulled his head back. Reuben endured it with eyes only for the plastic glass of water.

"Here you go!" Eugene said merrily, turning up the glass and aiming a stream at Reuben's mouth.

He struggled to catch it, then choked and angry, coughing, tried to yank his head away. But a laughing Eugene pulled him back by his hair and kept on pouring. It wasn't water. It was searing white rum that got in his eyes and burned his throat and sent him helplessly raging.

33

Nat Reybuhr waited with Tony Quayle outside the trailer while the makeup man examined the damage to Branwell Kane. He watched the security people coming back empty-handed. He wished he hadn't agreed to accompany the crew to this damned island. He needed a doctor. He no longer gave a damn about the script.

Beside him Tony Quayle tried to calm himself and control his elation and think of his heart. He called over his shoulder, "What's the word, Nick?"

The makeup man said from inside, "He's not bad. I can fix him up. The bruises will look like they came from Esme defending herself. When you get Zoe back you can go on shooting."

To Nat Reybuhr, getting Zoe back looked unlikely. "It's karma," he said. "First a crazy parrot, then a crazy wild man, and now the crazy director wants me to enlarge one of the parts."

"She what!?"

"That's right. She wants to diminish the slave hero and build up the Rastafari, if they can find him."

"She's out of her mind. I'll talk to her."

"But you've gotta admit, he was *something*."

* * *

Margarite Barbon slithered down with her back against the smooth trunk of the banyan tree that might have been the enormous gray flank of an elephant. She crouched at its base behind a cluster of hanging tendrils trying to root themselves, and saw she was sitting beside what looked like an extruded leg of a wrought-iron bench. The appetite of the island was as insatiable as she remembered. The trees, the tangled vines, everything like an enormous python waiting to swallow her up if she didn't watch out.

Who was the fellow? He was huge! All that hair! He was the living embodiment of all her nightmares, and she had to have him. Those clothes were nondescript enough, weren't they, to be the outfit of a seventeenth-century slave? Her brain was busy amending the script. The man was a visual triumph. The Rastafari could just appear, he wouldn't have to act.

She watched Branwell Kane lumber down the metal steps of the makeup trailer, rocking the flimsy structure, and stride off across the lawn, dragging a makeup napkin from around his neck and throwing it to the ground.

"Hey, you there!"

He was calling on the head of security. In his khaki uniform, hands on hips, the man turned from his crew and watched with a barely concealed smile the actor stalking toward him in pantaloons and white knee stockings, his wig in his hand.

The director watched them walk together toward the tables where the catering service, in the manner of the British, had set out tea for the cast and crew.

Beneath the banyan tree she smiled with satisfaction. "Sometimes if you let go," Quayle had said, "you'll get marvels." He was right. She had trusted an impulse and kept the cameras going and caught a terrific scene. Sur-real—those ad-lib lines, the appearance of the giant.

What did the giant Rastafari want with Zoe anyway? A ransom? They'd pay it. Use it as bait to pull him in. She would put the girl at risk if she had to. She saw Zoe's knowing little smile. Serve the little twit right, do her good, wipe that smirk off her pretty face.

An insect lighted on the director's arm and, distracted by its incredible colors, she tried to call up its name. There'd been a little song about it. But she caught herself. She mustn't look back. She took off her sandal and swiped the cheeky thing, smearing its colors across her arm.

Then instant regrets for a gratuitous act of destruction. But she reminded herself that after every triumph she suffered a bout of depression.

Señor Ribera leaned a shoulder against the table set up on sawhorses and covered with a paper tablecloth that reached the ground. He was savoring the fresh fruit salad. When nobody was looking, he'd stuffed his pockets with the tasty little rolls. Nobody else was eating. He had the spread to himself. The crew milled about, pointing to the woods, arguing, gesticulating. Something had happened, he wasn't sure what. He took little interest in this film business.

Except for the meals, he was fast growing bored. The Moors had made things interesting for a time. He'd meant to instruct them, show them who their enemies really were. Not the Spanish. Oh no. It was the Brits. They were still here, weren't they? Waited on hand and foot, doubtless by Moorish servants—that old house-keeper watching from the verandah.

But, alas, once back on the home island, Whatley had

left the group, and young Moss was only on hand now and then, mostly, it seemed, out of curiosity, just watching the goings-on.

Señor Ribera rose on tiptoes in white leather pumps chalky from many polishings, and eyed a stick of butter. He loved buttered rolls. But his pockets were full, and the climate too warm.

Señor Ribera wasn't equipped for such heat. His clothes weren't right. He was perspiring now through his linen jacket, but he daren't take it off. The rolls. He'd confiscated a few things from the costume trailer, but period pieces would hardly do. Still, the centuries-old styles appealed to him, the ruffled shirts. One day he'd find a use for them.

On tiptoe he reached with his fork and speared choice bits of turkey and ham from the big salad bowls dotting the middle of the table. Some never made it to his plate but went straight to the small pink mouth cradled by his trim dark beard. He frowned. The table was too high, the ground too uneven, and the butter fast melting. People were inconsiderate.

These *Americanos* had no sense of punctilio. They all dressed alike in short pants and sleeveless shirts. Like children, like little boys. You couldn't tell who was important and who was not.

Uh-oh, somebody coming.

A stealthy impulse in Señor Ribera's soul made him duck under the table with his mounded plate, accidentally knocking to the ground his ivory-headed cane, which he'd leaned against the leg of one of the sawhorses. He drew the cane in after him, then, sitting cross-legged on the grass, hidden by the long paper tablecloth with a border of flowers, he went on feasting.

It was Branwell Kane out there. Under the edge of the
cloth he could see the buckled shoes, the white knee
stockings. He heard Kane say, "A hundred thousand to
the man who brings her back, and it drops twenty thousand each day you fail."

Señor Ribera stopped eating. A hundred thousand *dollars*? His head swam with the enormity. A breeze ruffled
the tablecloth and he glimpsed the Jamaican head of
security as he hurried off shouting, "Get a Jeep up here!"

Then a hand pulled the tablecloth aside and Branwell
Kane bent down and smiled in at him. "Enjoying yourself, you little runt? Filling up that little round belly?"
And, laughing, Kane dropped the walls of Señor Ribera's
hiding place.

The little Spaniard sprang out from under the sawhorse
table, spilling his plate on the grass. He ran after the fat
actor, shaking his cane. "You pachyderm! Dinosaur!
Who're you to speak of bellies!"

Then rage gave way to grief and he slid back down in
his hiding place with his head in his hands, and wept with
self-pity for all his life's privations. When he could sob
no more, he crept out and reached for one of the pitchers
on the table. Full of ice and juice it was hard to lift, but
he managed, upending it with both hands. His throat
pulsed with pleasure as he drank. Ahhh, the *Americanos*
understood about juices. He closed his eyes and exhaled
with satisfaction.

Then he dreamily scratched his back against one of the
sawhorses, recalling an invitation from a Cuban woman
he'd met abroad. He'd get over there somehow. Too
bad the economy was in such a plight, but usually the
wealthy did not suffer. Cuba was only a little way across

the water, a short flight. Barring that, he would hire a boat. It was time to leave Jamaica.

First, he had to get his hands on some money.

34

Gabriel thrashed through the rain forest. Vines clutched him and branches lashed his face and caught his hair. He kept to the dense jungle, skirting the chine they'd cut for the road. He could hear the faint cries of brothers down there hawking their bird and turtle carvings to tourists sightseeing in their Japanese rental cars. To Zoe McNaire, doubled across his shoulder, they could have been walking the sea floor, so thin and green was the sunlight filtering through. His chest was heaving, she could feel it in the front of her thighs, and he stank of sweat.

She commenced again beating on his back, and he stopped in a clearing to rest and lifted her down in front of him. And Zoe, who spent whole nights terrified of intangibles, looked up at the giant and demanded, "What the hell do you think you're *do*ing!"

He was rescuing her, didn't she know that? She was such a little thing. Like a doll standing there glaring up at him. Not afraid of anything! A lot of people couldn't even look at him. Sometimes he liked the sense of power that gave him, and sometimes it made him pray Jah to make him invisible.

She reached to about the middle of his chest, pretty as a butterfly.

"Where are you taking me?"

He didn't know. Maybe to one of the villages. Maybe all the way to the Cockpits. They'd need horses for that. He knew where he could get some. Up there nobody would find them. She might be scared of him now but in the mountains she would see she was safe with him, rescued from the devils he'd caught mauling her. Then maybe she'd let him do more than look. It was all he could do now not to touch.

She eyed him. "You are something else, you know it?" She cocked her head and studied him. "I like your hair."

His shook his dreadlocks. " 'His head is as the most fine gold. His locks are bushy and black as a raven.' Solomon, five-eleven."

Cool. A wild man with a British accent quoting the Bible.

Then she did the unthinkable. She reached up and laid her fingers on his splayed lip.

He leapt back and grabbed her wrist.

"Let me go!"

He let her go.

"What," she said, "that harelip's your badge of honor or something?" He kept his silence while she studied his ruined face. "Why didn't they fix that when you were a baby?"

She held her wrist like it hurt, and he was ashamed of his hugeness, his roughness.

"You wouldn't be bad looking," she said, hands on her hips, "if they sewed that up. Now listen, you've got to let me go."

He saw again the scene back there on the grass, the fat man trying to do her. Why would she want to go back?

He stubbornly shook his head. " 'For the hurt of

the daughter of my people am I hurt.' Jeremiah, eight twenty-one."

"What's all this Bible crap?"

He frowned. "I am a locksman."

She couldn't make anything of that.

"I am a Rasta man."

"Oh, okay, right." Everybody knew about the Rasta-farians. "But you've got to take me back."

"You are safe now," he said. "Nobody will hurt you."

She studied him. The man was obviously messed in the head. She stepped back. When he reached out to grab her she spun around and made for the forest.

He laughed. It was like a game. He let her get a head start. No way could he lose her. He could hear every bit of headway she made, thrashing through the jungle with little cries of frustration at all the vines tripping her up. Finally he went after her. She hadn't got far. He found her lying in a tangle of growth, sobbing, hitting out at the vines, the undergrowth, the wall of green. He tried to free her, but she fought him.

"Quit now. Hole still," he said, producing his cane knife from where he wore it stuck in his belt under his loose shirt.

She screamed when she saw it. "What're you doing!" scurrying away but the trees had her. "Get away! Let me go!" She couldn't take her eyes off the knife. It was sharp and curved at the end.

But he went on pulling and hacking at the vines while she cringed with her eyes on the knife.

There. She was free. He let his arms fall and stepped back panting, looking at her with a grimace she took for a smile.

Rubbing welts on her arms from vines like snakes, like

living creatures bent on trapping her, it seemed to her that they were his allies, that all the time he'd spent in the woods had won him their allegiance. She lay there trying to think how she could get him to do what she wanted. Though they were bigger and stronger, she always found ways of controlling men.

But before she came up with a plan, he laughed with what sounded to her like delight, and picked her up and threw her over his shoulder again like a sack of yams. She yelled and beat on him with fists that felt to Gabriel like a child's. He stilled her legs against his chest and, slowed by the dense growth of the rain forest, made his way up the mountain.

And hanging upside down over his shoulder that way, when he bent to the climb and the tail of his shirt lifted, she saw the knife nestled in the small of his back, next to his coffee skin. She quieted down. She would bide her time.

35

The plantation house was old, and filled with light in spite of the shade trees outside. Margarite Barbon let the screen fall to behind her and stood in the broad center hall, taking in the spacious rooms. Fans turned soundlessly in the high ceilings. It was very familiar, a typical old frame plantation house that would creak and sway in the tropical storms that swept the island.

Ever since arriving on the set, she had avoided intruding here. Yet there on the crest of the hill the house had loomed in her consciousness.

The light in the hallway was green, muted by the deep verandah screened by vines. There was the moist smell of flowers and fresh-cut grass and recent rain. Stairs circled to a landing and turned, making for the upper floor.

She stood hesitantly in the breezeway bisecting the house, the airy living room on her left, the dining room with a banquet table on her right. The dining room furniture was dark mahogany, but elsewhere the furnishings were light, mostly wicker or bamboo, the cushions covered in pale floral prints. The floors were wide polished boards. Everywhere she looked, the house echoed a decided taste.

She's been entertaining the possibility that, now the old lady was dead, maybe the husband could be talked into letting them use the plantation house for interiors— for a price, of course, and if they could find him. The contract had excluded it, but it would save the cost of building sets back in the Hollywood studios, and save more money by saving time.

On a table in the parlor beside an armchair lay a pair of thick glasses on a cord. She knew without knowing how that they had belonged to the plantation's dead mistress Charlotte, Dame of the British Empire. A fitting title for a powerful old lady who knew her own mind. She recalled the dead eyes staring accusingly.

Books lay open facedown on top of one another on the hassock. The director moved quietly into the room and read the titles on the spines: *Outstation Nursing*, *Bovine Husbandry*, *The Harvesting of Spices*. Apparently the lady had been involved in every aspect of the plantation.

Nostalgia lodged in her throat. Not many of these old houses left. Most were long since nothing more than mounds of rubble claimed by the tropics. She wondered how this one had survived the uprisings. Probably it hadn't, but had at some point been rebuilt.

She had crept inside to see the place and discover what changes would have to be made if her plan was to work, and also—if she could avoid that old tyrant of a house-keeper—to locate a quiet escape from the chaos on the lawns. She wanted to map out a few scenes without Zoe McNaire that could be filmed tomorrow, taking the place of those she had planned.

She turned from the parlor to the dining room, where she might work with her production book at the dining room table. She might even yet get a take before dark.

And tomorrow the scene of the governor's horsemen, swords drawn, thundering down on the cane field. She could ready that one quickly. The horses had been brought in and pastured somewhere back in the plantation fields. She expected to have to do the scene more than once to get it right. She'd try it tomorrow and capture later on the slave extras fleeing in terror. More people in that one, more preparation. Take them running in panic—close-ups of faces—the sound of the horses and the shouts of the governor's men dubbed over. That should do it. Be very effective, in fact. Sometimes you got your best shots when you had to improvise. She must find the cinematographer.

Turning, she almost passed over the sofa, but there her eyes snagged. A glimpse, like déjà vu, and something strange was happening. She put her hand to her head. She frowned, tried to turn away, but the sofa held her like a magnet capable of snaring flesh. She backed away with a feeling like fright.

And suddenly the smell of flowers and rain and rich black earth threatened her equilibrium. This past year dim memories had begun surfacing, some so frightening she couldn't believe they were actual memories. Her shrink had warned the director against coming to this place. But Margarite Barbon had shrugged that off, even ridiculed the idea that she would give up this film out of nebulous fears. She was strong, she said. She could handle it.

But here in this room suddenly she felt faint. She knew this place. She'd been here before. She backed away from the sofa till up against the wall she could go no farther. She laid her head back and closed her eyes and her lips moved rapidly.

Consciousness didn't slip slowly away, it fled all at once. When slowly she came to someone was holding her, cradling her and crooning softly, no words she could distinguish though the patois was all too familiar. Feeling vulnerable and afraid there on the polished floor, she tried to rise, but he whispered, "Weh-t, weh-t, you are all right. Be easy now."

She opened her eyes and was flooded with relief. Thank God it wasn't Quayle or Branwell Kane but Datrey Moss, the gentle young novelist, who smiled sweetly down at her. Over them both stood a light-skinned woman in an apron with a purple rag around her head, holding a wooden kitchen spoon.

"I'm all right now," the director said, and pulled away, but Datrey Moss didn't let her go. He held on and helped her up.

"So sorry . . ." she said, "so embarrassing."

"Are you all right?" he asked anxiously, keeping an arm around her.

"Yes . . . fine. I'm not sure what happened."

"You fainted," he said. "This is Claire Falway, the woman who raised me."

"Oh, your mother."

"We were in the kitchen. We heard you fall. Have you hurt yourself?" He touched her cheek.

She drew back. "Maybe I hit my head falling."

"You've had a shock," the woman Claire Falway said, "mebbe you ought to teh-k a minute and lay yourself down." With the long-handled spoon she indicated the sofa.

"No! No, please don't trouble yourselves. I'm quite all right." She sidled toward the big double archway to the hall.

Datrey Moss followed with his arms out to catch her if she stumbled. "So sorry to hear of the misfortune," he said.

It took her a minute to think which misfortune.

"It had to be Gabriel," he said.

Uncomprehending, she looked at him.

"The man with the ruined feh-ce," he said. "The one took your lovely star."

The confused feelings of the past few moments fled. *"You know him?"*

Datrey Moss smiled. "Oh, yes. We all know him."

"Where would he take Zoe?" She felt sure her wild man would follow no track that Jeeps could manage. No. He would keep to the dense woods. He was sure to know them much better than the coastal men of the security guard.

For a moment the young writer studied her. Then he shrugged. "Perhaps to Negril," he said. "But I doubt it. Probably he would make for the ruinate or the Cockpit country."

The Cockpits. She hadn't thought of them. The landscape of the moon! God, she had to work in more shots of that bizarre place than the script called for. As soon as she'd thought it, it was no longer a wish but a necessity. Plans for the afternoon went on hold.

"Could you take me there?"

Datrey Moss considered her solemnly. Finally he nodded. "I will teh-k you, yes. If it doesn't rain."

36

But it did. It started pouring and flooded down like a cloud sluice had opened, no sign it would ever stop. Zoe and Gabriel were soaked. The rain would have barely penetrated the canopy of trees, but before it started the forest had ended. The edge was so abrupt, the line of it so straight it was as if a giant cutlass had sliced it away.

The cane sloped upward in ranks. Gabriel slipped and slid across the wet rutted track that ran along its edge. He strode ahead now, no longer afraid she would run—where would she run to? And even if she ran he could easily catch her. Once across the track, he broke into what seemed a solid barrier of cane, and looking back, smiling to encourage her, made his way ahead so he could brush the sharp-edged cane leaves aside and make way for her to follow.

They had barely left the road and were hidden in the cane when the sound of a motor rose. Listening, he grabbed her and held her still. When the motor neared and slowed, its wheels spinning on the slick track, he pulled her down in a cane row and folded himself over her, listening.

"Damn you!" she said. "You've got me muddy!"

He put his big hand over her mouth.

But the motor passed. It had slowed only for the rising ground and the slippery road. It sounded old. It chugged with effort. Pleased it hadn't been a patrol, about to rise he felt her body beneath him and hesitated. Then the pleasure of his unexpected arousal, the pressure of it against her, caused him to lift himself slightly and look down at her.

And taking in the wealth of her hair, the beauty of her face, he encountered a taunting smile and his cane knife turned in her hand with the blade toward him.

Poised for another second with his elbows straddling her, he braced on one and grabbed for the knife. His hand closed over the blade and she jerked it up. His blood spurted all over her clothes, her face. He rolled off her onto his back on the cane leaves left by the cutters, clutching his hand. She sat up and leaned frowning over him. He looked up at her, surprised, and with hurt feelings clasped his bleeding hand to his chest.

She put the blade to his throat. "You were going to rape me!"

He turned his head, ashamed. "No woman no cry," he whispered.

She was surprised. She recognized the line from the Bob Marley song. She looked from the hand bleeding all over his chest, to the knife she was holding. She lapsed back on her heels.

"Promise you won't hurt me."

His forehead ridged with worry, he raised his head and nodded, then let it drop.

She considered a moment, then threw down the knife and tore the ruffle off the hem of her costume skirt.

"Here," she said. "Let me see."

He opened his eyes and relinquished the hand. She

spread the black fingers and frowned at the pink palm red with his blood. "It's deep."

"Yes." The first sharp pain had passed into an aching numbness.

She wound the ruffle around his hand, then folded his fingers over his palm and wound his fist tightly with the rest of the ruffle. She sat back on her heels and looked at him. He rolled over and with his good hand picked up the knife.

She gasped. "You promised!"

He turned the hilt and held it out to her. She shook her head. "No! I don't want it." She shoved it away.

He looked down at his prized possession, then reared back and threw it as far as he could over the heads of the cane.

The overcast was gone. They walked the cane aisle his head barely topped. The rain had stopped. The sky with little white powder-puff clouds looked washed. The sun was lower on the horizon. Then the cane abruptly ended and it was forest again, though not so dense. They walked up a deep-rutted track with jungle pressing in on either side. Sounds came from up ahead, and he glanced over his shoulder to reassure her.

She heard the village long before they reached it—at first just drums, then a hound baying, then dogs barking, and closer, the gabble of chickens quarreling. They rounded a bend in the forest track, and there it was.

A white goat strained at its tether to get at a bush across the stream. A boy chased a rooster that fled squawking with its wings spread, iridescent red and gold and a black that was blue in the sunlight, everything dripping after the rain. And along with the smell of rain, the sound of water. It was everywhere—cascading alongside the path, over rocks in the stream, pearled on the leaves, and from somewhere the sound of falls.

They came into the clearing. Chickens scattered and dogs came out from under the houses and growled with their ears back. Zoe froze, surrounded.

Women along the stream left off slapping their wash on rocks to look at them. Gabriel greeted people by name. They nodded, with eyes only for the stranger.

A woman with a bowl in the circle of her arm and another one balanced on a folded cloth on top of her head stopped in the path, and the child running to keep up stuck out her stomach and clung to the woman's legs. A man picked up a stick and said something, and Zoe waited to see if the stick was for her or for the dogs. Relieved when the curs crept back under houses, she moved forward again with Gabriel beside her, less afraid of him now that she had something that seemed to shame him.

The houses sat up on piles of stones—flat gray slabs of rock stacked to uneven heights to accommodate the tilt of the land, giving the houses a cockeyed aspect. The flat rock slabs also served as steps and stepping stones, for where the pigs rooted and the chickens pecked away the grass, the earth turned slick and muddy after rains.

The houses were nothing but shacks, she saw, made out of whatever came to hand—the slab sides of lumber with the bark still on, corrugated metal eaten by rust, saplings woven together with vines, concrete blocks, Coca-Cola signs, fenders and doors off old cars. But what struck Zoe was all the color against the forest's green—the reds and oranges and blues of clothes on the lines, or vividly set off by the black limbs of the women and children, and the riot of flowers, and blue water flowing like music over stream-washed boulders.

All those eyes made her uneasy. They walked on. At some distance off the drums still beat. The man with the stick muttered something over his shoulder, and an old woman with rheumy eyes crept out of the house behind him and looked out at them from her door.

Gabriel hailed her. "How you, ol' momma?"

"I be very fine, bwai," the old woman said. "What this you brought us?"

He stepped behind Zoe and picked her up and set her down on one of the limestone steps to the old woman's rotting porch.

The old woman came closer. She was very black with a red rag around her head. "Well, I be! She sweet as the cane!"

Zoe wondered if they were making fun of her. A hand black and gnarled as a root touched her cheek, arm, breast. "She a little light-skinned thing! Who be her mam?"

Zoe stood still under the exploring hand. "My mother's in California."

The old woman turned near-blind eyes in Gabriel's direction. "What she say?" For Zoe didn't talk the talk of the island.

"Say her mam ain here."

A barefoot child chased a chicken around the corner of a house and, seeing Zoe, stopped and put a finger in his mouth. More children crept out for a look at her. A little one, frightened, screwed up his face and turned on his sister's hip and let out a squall.

The woman with the bowl said coldly, "What are you thinking, to bring this up here!"

Gabriel said, "Hold yuh tongue, Leesha."

"She don't belong here!"

"She one of us."

"You wrong."

Zoe was hurt. In spite of the poverty, there was some richness here. All the doors were open, everybody seemed to know everybody else, the children seemed to belong to the whole village. She realized with suddenness and shock that all her life she'd been lonely.

But even as she looked longingly at the women by the stream, she scoffed at herself and applied her mantra: She was rich, she was famous, people she didn't even know were in love with her, she had everything.

The woman with the bowl said, "What's your name, girl?"

Zoe wasn't used to being addressed so brazenly. The woman's head was erect on her long neck, regal under the other bowl she carried up there. Her skin had a reddish cast, and the bones of her face were finely made.

"Zoe," she said. And louder, with a touch of arrogance, "My name is Zoe."

The old woman said, "That a name I never stumble across. What kind of a name is that?"

Zoe said she thought it was Greek. The old woman guffawed, revealing two teeth in her lower jaw, one on either side of a gaping middle. "It be Greek to this old head!"

The comment released laughter that had apparently been damned up waiting. Though the woman with the bowl didn't join in, her child's face broke open with a smile, which she quickly hid in her mother's skirts.

"Travelers must be thirsty," the tall woman said, distant, cold, but as if she remembered some manners of the place that must be observed.

Zoe said yes, she was.

"Set down yuh cotta, Leesha," the old woman said, "an bring this child somethin."

While Gabriel inquired about horses, Zoe let herself be led to a porch with edges bitten and green with mold. A boy in ragged pants bent over the stream and retrieved an Orange Crush from behind a rock dam. Now she saw that the stream tumbling down was crossed at intervals of a few feet by rock dams, and in the eddies behind them melons and six-packs of beer were chilling. How clever, she thought: the village uses the stream for its refrigerator. She took the Orange Crush gratefully.

"Ain no horses here," the man told Gabriel. "They dragging timber. They won't be back till evenin."

Gabriel frowned, looking back the way they'd come. She could tell he was afraid they'd be followed. She was relieved that they couldn't go on. She liked this place. She wasn't afraid of him here in the village. The stop was a reprieve. It would give her time to think. She had to escape. Margarite Barbon would be spitting bricks. But she had worked at Esme all morning, been snatched up and carried through an inpenetrable forest by an ugly giant, and defended herself with a knife. She was tired. All she wanted was to sit with the women by the stream and put her feet in the water.

37

The market swirled around him vivid as confetti, but Señor Ribera—all in white: suit, vest, shoes, panama hat—stood planted there with both hands propped in front of him on top of his ivory-headed cane. The crowd shouted greetings over his head, met and squabbled and broke around him like a wave on a rock. Señor Ribera was not deterred. He was making up his mind.

He approached the stand of a woman selling fresh fruit from her garden. She was a tall stout woman, and he usually avoided people of large stature, especially women, but this one wore the stamp of authority. He'd watched long enough to see that the other sellers treated her with deference.

"Madam," he said, looking straight ahead at her ample midriff, "do you know of anyone here in the market for valuables?"

It was late in the day and the fruit seller had begun packing her baskets to head back to her village. She looked down at the little man and her face opened with delight.

"Why, jes look at you!" she exclaimed. "Ain you a cute little thing!"

"Madam," he said, his eyes traveling up her bosom, up

the proud dark column of neck to fix on a broadly smiling face, "I assure you I am not *cute*."

"Well, I think you dahlin," she said. "What you buying? Heah, try this. Have a papaw."

Before he could object she'd placed a thin, dripping custard of green, like the sweetest of hosts, between his startled lips.

What happened then had never happened to Señor Ribera before. As if the thing really were imbued with divine powers, with all its sweetness dribbling down his chin, and the fruit seller beaming upon him with appreciation of his uniqueness, he felt a weakness begin at his center and spread to all his parts. And though it threatened his hard-won manly dignity, he was unable to draw himself up and assert the profound sense of separateness, of isolation, that was his bulwark against the intrusions of pity or curiosity. Instead, he felt an inexplicable desire to fall upon that bosom and be folded in those massive arms.

The fruit seller bent over him, cupping a hand to her ear. "Tell Bernice again what you looking for."

Threatened by the strange impulse, he drew back, ripped his handkerchief from his breast pocket, wiped the sweetness off his beard, and asked in a firm loud voice, "Does anyone here trade in valuables?"

Out of nowhere a shadow loomed over him, shutting out the sun. Señor Ribera found himself facing a knotted rope supporting a pair of dusty trousers so loose they gathered in pleats around the wearer's narrow hips. Again his eyes began their ascent, traveling up over a multicolored shirt tight on a sunken chest, and up farther to a smile marked by the white of tooth and eye and set in a wealth of wild matted locks.

"I knows somebody buys play-pritties," the man said.

"Rat this way. If you will please to follow me." The stranger bowed from the waist, an act so respectful it flattered Señor Ribera and won his confidence.

His guide set off through the crowd, smiling back to see that he followed, and turned at a little distance up a side alley with Señor Ribera scurrying after.

"Don't go up that alley, little man!" the fruit seller called.

But Señor Ribera ignored her and hurried as fast as his short legs could carry him after the wild head disappearing in the crowd.

The fruit seller cried out again, "Listen to Bernice, little man! Don't go up that alley!"

But anxious to escape the debilitating power exerted over him by the fruit seller, and feeling safe now under masculine guidance, Señor Ribera hurried on.

38

The first time he surfaced, he thought he was floating high up and looking down on a field of white flowers, some of them large and some so small and distant they all ran together.

The next time he opened his eyes he knew he was lying on his back on a hard surface and looking not down but *up* at a field of stars in a soft night sky. There weren't so many now as there had been, they were dimmed by the light of the rising moon.

His head hurt. He wanted to touch it but that was awkward with his hands still tied. But his nose itched and he was able to scratch it. At least now they were tied in front of him.

Then he was aware of sounds he couldn't identify: maybe a dog growling, a voice muttering, though he couldn't make out any words. And something else.

Drums.

With the rhythm of a heartbeat they lulled him back into a heavy drugged sleep. Some time later when he woke again, the drums were so close he thought he could feel their vibrations. And in the distance other drums he imagined echoing across wet green valleys he thought he had seen, but it must have been in a dream.

Still later he was drawn reluctantly to consciousness by the smell of meat cooking. With his headache, the smell made him nauseous. He vomited and rolled away to keep from fouling himself. He tasted the rum they'd poured down him on the pirate ship. All he remembered after that was his head swinging on his chest and his bare toes dragging in the sand. They were carrying him, one on each arm. And a man's voice, ". . . never could hold his . . ." People laughing, and him unable to lift his head or speak.

His gorge rose again. But the night air was cool, and he kept still and it subsided. He could see now out of both eyes, but one of them hurt. Had somebody hit him? He couldn't remember.

An unearthly glow lit the tropical night. Where had they brought him? What was this place? He was lying on something hard and slanty. He ran his bound hands over the surface, exploring. Sand fine as powder covered a surface smooth and gently ridged, as if scoured and hardened by waves.

He rolled onto his side and winced, his hip felt badly bruised, and up swam the memory of a wild ride on a hard seat, maybe an old Jeep, nothing to hang onto. Somebody reached back and held him. "Whoa! Slow down! You'll pitch him out if you not careful!"

"Serve him right."

He made himself stay awake. Subtle explorations confirmed that he was lying in a rock depression shaped like a Frisbee, one side shadowed, the other faintly lit. He listened to a voice rhythmically rising and falling. And the drums. He rolled up on his knees and crawled to the saucer's lip and peered over.

His first thought was he'd been abducted by aliens.

And his second: They've taken me beyond the realms of possibility.

If he laughed it would hurt, so he didn't laugh. He had to be hallucinating. He wanted to shake his head to clear it, but what if his brain went one way and his skull another? So he lay back in solid rock shaped like a hammock, and smelled meat cooking. That had to be real.

Presently his nausea fled and left him hungry. He pulled himself close to the lip and squinted out at a landscape of low rounded hills and, nearer, depressions like pockmarks on the surface of a planet. It looked like maybe it would look if he were marooned on the moon.

But that was the moon, wasn't it, poised over there on a hard-edge horizon, huge as he'd never seen it, bigger than the little earth. And in its light, everything—the wavering curve of horizon it sat on, the soft velvet sky— was black or shades of gray, except for, off a little way behind him, a paler circle of light.

He turned and focused on that ring of light, and at last saw something familiar—a white dog with yellow spots lying on its side with its feet out, growling now and then in its sleep.

The light came from a fire burning in a round depression bigger than his. It turned the faces of the men sitting around it red as copper.

Some heavy animal hung over the fire on a makeshift spit—forked branches laced together and spanned by a sagging limb. As he watched, a knife reached out and cut off a strip of the meat. The men in the circle around the fire were eating meat off their knives while an old man stood up in the middle, muttering with his head back to the beat of a drum keeping time with a metallic clack like rim shots. It was like the music of some gravely solemn rap musician.

He was shivering. He wanted to crawl toward the fire. He couldn't hug himself with his hands tied like that, so he brought his arms close to warm his chest and discovered he was naked but for the blue swim trunks. They had dried, and the elastic waist band cut into him like he'd put on weight.

He discovered his feet were free. He thought of running. But no idea where he was, or where he wanted to go. And the smell of the meat made him hungry.

Hands commenced a ragged clapping. Others joined in. The old man's voice rose and fell. Now he saw the drummer. He had on a knit cap and he beat with a stick on what looked like the lid of a tar bucket. That accounted for the metallic sound.

Some wore long sleeves, some wore no shirts. Some wore dreadlocks, some didn't. One in the back row with bare muscled arms crossed over his chest had on a tweed cap with a little bill straight out of Dickens, and the man next to him wore a black felt fedora with the brim chewed around the edges. A man directly across the fire had a watch cap pulled down to his eyebrows. They all listened intently as the old man chanted. One lens of his eyeglasses was cracked diagonally. They reflected the light and hid his eyes. In spiky dreadlocks and a shirt with the sleeves ripped off at the shoulders, and old faded cutoffs, he moved to the rhythm of the drum. It was hypnotic. Reuben dozed. Then the drum and chanting stopped, jerking him awake. With the weight of authority, the old man pointed an accusing finger at one of the men sitting around the fire.

Reuben squinted with his good eye. The man sitting

there with his arms hanging loosely off his knees, in jeans and a long-sleeved shirt with the cuffs flapping, was the bridegroom, Simon.

"They tell me somebody kill her," the old man said, his voice surprisingly strong for his slight frame.

Simon nodded. "That is what they say." He reached in his shirt pocket and took out a long cheroot and put a stick in the fire to light it. Something arrogant and proud in the gesture made the old man rear up, affronted. Expressionless, the others watched.

"They tell me you the one accused!"

Simon drew on the cigar and tossed the stick back in the fire. "That may be true."

The old man's legs in the stringy cutoffs were as thin and knobby as a stork's. At the end of a ropy arm his pointing finger shook. Clearly he was an authority. "They say you have run from the law!"

Simon nodded and launched an elongating string of spittle toward the fire. "Yes. For their prisons are barracoons. If they lay hold of a black man they never let him go."

"Stand up, Simon," the old man commanded, his finger pointing at the stone ground in front of him.

With what looked like reluctance, Simon pulled himself to his feet and stood much taller than the old man. The others around the fire watched intently.

"Simon, I will put it to you once," the old man said. "Have you loss your sense an kill the old lady?"

A man Reuben recognized leapt to his feet and demanded, "Would he kill his motha?" looking around the circle of faces.

Simon said softly, "Sit down, Eugene."

Eugene fell back and sat with his legs out in front

of him and his arms crossed over his chest, looking at
the fire.

"Why would I go and kill the leh-dy?" Simon asked in
his deep voice, tapping the ash off the cigar, putting it
back in his mouth and just this side of insolence looking
down at the oldster.

The man struck Reuben as insufferable. It wasn't that
he was black, was it? And had the background, the assurance, the education, and yes even the damned British
accent, while he himself was a self-taught painter from
an outlying borough of New York City, a Jew, a latter-
day fauve whose colors announced themselves with
shouts.

If that was it, so be it, he'd take it, it was who he was.

Eugene said eagerly, "Why he kill her? Ever'thin
belong to him soon enough anyway."

Simon said softly, "Hush, Eugene."

Was this a kangaroo court? Who was this oldster?
Some kind of chief or obeah man?

Simon removed the cigar and tapped off the ash.
Crouching, Reuben squinted with his good eye, searching
the faces. Some looked in the fire, some at the old man,
none looked at Simon. What did that mean?

"They say you argue and fight with the leh-dy, and she
rebuke you."

"Who told you that?"

Eugene bounced once and exclaimed, "He the heir!
You know it!"

Simon said softly, "Eugene, shut your mouth."

Suddenly Eugene pointed across the fire, and Reuben
ducked but not fast enough. Crouched with his back to
them he heard Simon say, "Well now, what do you
know? Our guest is a-weh-k."

Reluctantly, Reuben looked up. He felt low and vulnerable there in the shallow pit wearing nothing but swim trunks, with his hands tied and Simon standing over him.

"It was not I who killed her," Simon said, smiling down at him. "But I have brought you the one who did."

Reuben squinted up at him smoking his cheroot. "You're crazy," he croaked, then found his voice. "Why would I want to kill her?"

Simon smiled, his face cruel in the light and shadows. "Because you were paid to. You belong to The Man."

Reuben sank back against the rock. Here was one more perk of the fucking job.

"He is what I believe is called in the Steh-tes 'a hit man,' " Simon said, and drew on the cigar.

Reuben's laugh came out a wheeze.

"They paid him to kill Charlotte, and now they have sent him after me."

It was another setup, this time the killer the accuser. He preferred the police. He looked Simon in the eye with his one good one. He looked around at the men. Eyes watchful, they moved closer.

"He's lying! Don't buy this shit!"

Simon squatted to his level and chuckled, their faces close, and balanced the cigar on the lip of the pit. Then his free hand grabbed Reuben by his short beard and sliced.

"Hey!" Reuben knocked the knife away with his bound-together hands.

The smell was like chickens singed clean in his grandmother's Long Island backyard. He swiped at a dribble of blood down his chin. "You goddam creep!" The man had cut off his beard and skin that came with it and thrown them in the fire.

"And now," Simon said, "you will tell me which one of them paid you to murder her in her sleep."

Reuben closed his eyes. He felt dizzy. With his empty stomach and the smell of his beard and the sting where he'd lost skin, his gorge rose and he was at pains to control it.

Simon picked up the cigar and calmly drew on it. The tip flared. He blew the smoke in Reuben's face. Reuben dodged and spit out bile that rose in his throat with the taste of rum. They must have put something in it. Then the cigar's burning tip came toward him, and he clubbed at it awkwardly with his bound fists.

Simon smiled and put it back between his teeth. "Hand me the puppy." His eyes on Reuben, he reached behind him.

Reuben glanced nervously at the yellow and white spotted dog, but what they put in Simon's hand was a small chrome pistol.

Simon said, "This is your judge and jury," indicating the others.

Reuben looked. Their faces were terra-cotta in the light.

"Simon, weh-t," the old man said.

"I honor you, William," Simon said, "but the murderer will pay."

Reuben was cold but he was sweating, then the sweat was also cold.

Simon said, "You have one chance, hit man. If you would save your life, tell me who paid you to murder Charlotte."

"Come on! You know I didn't kill her! You can't just . . ." But here on a mountaintop in the dead of night, the man could probably do anything he wanted.

"Tell us who," Simon said, and raised the pistol. Reuben swung with his bound hands and knocked it away from a startled Simon. It clattered across the pit. That gave him courage. He rose to a crouch, then to his feet. He'd never been in a fight in his life, but maybe the Oxford scholar hadn't either. And his own center of gravity was better located than the lanky Jamaican's.

Simon's hand shot out, caught Reuben's bound wrists and with a twist forced him over on his side. He rolled away from a vicious kick and swung around and grabbed Simon's arm with his bound-together hands, toppling him also into the pit. He tried to get up but Reuben kicked his feet out from under him. Then—both on their knees, then on their feet—they circled each other.

The crowd on the lip watched like watching a cockfight, only peculiarly quiet. The one voice cheering Simon on was Eugene's. Simon lashed out and Reuben's head snapped back and he bit his tongue. Then Simon got set to spring. But tasting blood Reuben leapt in one motion up the side of the saucer and brought down his bound hands, chopping the back of Simon's neck. Simon fell clutching Reuben around the chest, then the shoulders. Then his hands found his throat.

Reuben couldn't breathe. Pressure swelled behind his eyes. He fell over backward with Simon on top of him, planting his knees for leverage. With a last surge of effort, Reuben rammed his knee into the bridegroom's crotch, and Simon fell over screaming and clutching himself.

Reuben's breath rushed back, filled the vacuum of his lungs, and he scrambled up on one knee like a runner awaiting the gun. Sweat dripped off his nose and chin, he panted, but the daily runs and workouts were paying off, and swinging his bound hands low in front of him like he knew what he was doing, he crouched, daring the others.

When nobody moved, he sprang up and sprinted across the pit and picked up the pistol and flung it as far as he could into the dark, then spun around to meet them coming. Still nobody moved.

Then Eugene shouted, "Here Gabriel now!"

Reuben turned. He shook his head. He must be hallucinating again. Sitting astride a swayback white horse emerging from the dark and clip-clopping toward them came Zoe McNaire.

39

"What do you mean gettin back this late?" Jane Boll demanded. "I never heard you come in!"

But Matilde hadn't been inside. On the side porch, illumined by the soft yellow light from the tall windows, she glided dreamily in the hammock, twirling a scarlet hibiscus in her fingers.

"That's because you sound asleep on the sofa, Auntie."

"Don't be facy wid me! Where you been all this time?"

Matilde wasn't about to tell. Her hand trailed languidly to pluck a magenta bougainvillea blossom creeping through the banisters. Out in the garden the macaw complained in his sleep.

"Cyain trust you young folks now'days. I will have to send you home to Montego Bay," Jane grumbled, letting herself down in a wicker rocker.

Earlier in the day, that would have been a boon instead of a threat, but things had changed. "Oh, please, Auntie, let me stay. I've been a good girl. I've done everything you asked!"

"Humph," Jane said. "You think I don't know what you up to?"

Matilde was alarmed. She harbored the superstition that old women had second sight.

"Ain up to nothing, Auntie!" Then she added softly, "Auntie?"

Jane softened. The girl was a pretty little thing. Not much upstairs, but sweet to look at with that clear coffee skin and lean young body.

"What is it, child?"

"Tell me bout the bridegroom."

Jane said sternly, "Don't waste your dreaming on Simon. He's above you. He smaht and educated, and now I spose he the riches black man on this island."

Matilde nodded. "Umm-hmm. Because Dame Charlotte she daid."

"How come you asking questions bout Simon?"

"Why he marry that old woman?"

"That a long story, girl, and none of your business."

"I loves your stories, Auntie. I could listen to you all night."

Flattered, Jane Boll chuckled. "Well, once upon a time . . ."

"No tell me bedtime tales, Auntie."

"Ain no tale, girl, this the truth. When Charlotte kick ole Major outa her bed he went to a fufu girl. B'time Charlotte take him back, that hussy gret wid child. Ole Major he tell her he acknowledge the babe if she go away, and that the last heard of the matter."

"What's that got to do with Simon marrying that old woman?"

"Watch your mouth, girl! Charlotte make a dozen of you!"

"I think I know," Matilde said slyly, weaving the

bougainvillea into a wreath for her hair. "He know she soon be dead. Then he rich, he marry anybody he like."

"Don't be a fool, girl. Simon never marry you!"

Matilde was so insulted she broke the promise she'd given in exchange for the trinket. "Ain no fool, Auntie!" she said. "Looky here." She pulled from her bosom and held out on her palm what Jane Boll could not believe she was looking at. It was Charlotte's cameo brooch.

"Ain nothin wrong wid it but a broken clasp," Matilde said, and cradled it lovingly between her palms.

40

The lieutenant had brought Perdita surprising news. He sat on the hearth and explained it all. She thought he'd been extremely clever. He reminded her a little of that TV detective she liked—hair, mustache, the circumflex eyebrows—the one with the legs.

When he left she sat holding the phone in her lap, thinking. She felt like something dreadful had come to a close and ought to be marked.

"You silly old hag."

Perdita smiled, remembering.

Charlotte was sitting at her dressing table in the airy, high-ceilinged room with the fan silently turning, dusting herself liberally with powder even as she lightheartedly chastised her image in the mirror.

Perdita, sitting behind her on the bed, had fallen in love with the old frame plantation house, its joints rattled loose by hurricanes. The light in the rooms was cream and green, muted by the bougainvillea that screened the verandah—the downstairs porch wrapping around the house; the one upstairs was the gallery.

It was the only time Perdita had visited Charlotte in Jamaica. Saxe-Ogilvy had returned from a shoot some days after she'd arrived. Not till then did she glimpse the truth of that marriage. She'd broken her natural reticence.

"Why have you stayed with him, Charlotte?"

"I'm stubborn."

"That you are."

"Hate's as good a mortar as love."

"You're wrong, Lottie."

"Usually." Charlotte watched herself laugh in the mirror. "He's older than I am. I'll outlive him."

"Is it some kind of contest?"

"I want the plantation."

"You, Charlotte, *cupidity*?"

"I will have paid for it."

"But at what a price."

"I have my reasons, old friend."

The lights on the scene flickered out. Presently Perdita called her servant. "Mix a shaker of your excellent martinis, Jack. And bring some of those good little biscuits."

She snapped her fingers at the wolf sleeping on the window seat behind her and his soft pads hit the floor. He sidled up and put his head under her hand.

"Wolf, give me strength," she said. "I'm going to need it."

41

Just outside the firelit circle the dog sat with its head cocked, looking up curiously at the white horse. The horse stretched out a foreleg and lowered its nose to the level of the creature at its feet and sniffed it all over. And the dog rose and danced on its hind legs, paddling the air with happy yelps that expressed what Reuben felt at his reprieve.

Now he sat in the circle around the fire, glad of the warmth, eating strips of the cooked meat off the end of a borrowed knife. Zoe sat beside him. The big man with the splayed-open lip and one hand wrapped in a dirty rag squatted protectively behind her, watching him suspiciously and making him uncomfortable.

The whole thing was otherworldly—the Cockpits, the drums in the distance, the unreal stars and the gigantic moon. Famished, he wolfed down the delicious meat.

"What *is* this?" he asked, turning it on the end of the knife.

"It's pig, mahn."

The wild pig they made jerked meat out of. It gave Reuben pause—they never ate pork at home—then he went on eating.

Simon sat across the fire with his arms hanging off his

jutting knees. Somebody had retrieved the gun and it rested in front of him. "If what you say is true, why are you following *me*?"

"Perdita asked me to find you."

"What for does she want to find me?"

"She wants you to bring Dame Charlotte's body home to Jamaica for burial." He put down the knife. "My head is killing me." He looked around at the faces. "Has anybody got an aspirin?" He thought it unlikely.

Somebody put a tin cup in his hand. "Drink."

But he thought of the drugged rum and shoved it away.

"Hit better than aspirin, mahn," Eugene said.

He hurt all over. He eyed the cup, then took it in both hands and sniffed it. He shrugged and drank it down. It tasted like some kind of herb tea.

Simon said, "If you are lying I will kill you."

Zoe McNaire laid a warning hand on Simon's arm and said, "Don't be silly. He had nothing to do with that business. I know. I was there. He was nowhere near the murder bedroom."

Reuben refrained from looking at her. Why would she lie for him? She'd been nowhere around while he packed the Caddy.

"He's an artist, not a murderer," she said.

"An artist are you!" William exclaimed. "Do you carve figures?"

Reuben shook his head, still working on the meat. "I paint landscapes." He knew some would argue with that.

"Our artists are poor. Most become carvers," William said, "for wood is plentiful."

Simon said, "If I didn't kill her and you didn't kill her, we are left with the question: Who killed Charlotte?"

If the man's innocence was an act, it was a good one. Reuben said, "How would I know?"

"Then we must find out."

Eugene said, "How we do that?"

Simon looked thoughtfully at the pig on the spit. He cut himself a strip off the carcass and took his time eating it, then wiped his fingers on the front of his shirt, reached out, and took hold of Zoe's arm. "We will go down to the plan-*teh*-tion and we will ask."

Gabriel put his arm around Zoe and closed his good hand over Simon's head. "Let go, bredda, before I crush you."

Simon said, "We're in your debt, Gabriel. You've brought us a prize. They can't do without her down there. While they weh-t to get her back, the Yankee dollar trickles away." He smiled at Zoe. "Americans are fond of their dollars, isn't that so? They will do anything to get you back. They will tell us what we want to know. If they don't, you will never go back."

Zoe said, "Come on, you don't scare me." Though he did, a little.

"And in that case she is yours, bruh. You can keep her here in the Cockpits, build you a little house, meh-k her comfortable. You'd like that, wouldn't you."

Zoe knocked his hand off but he caught her wrist.

"And while we go down there and ask our question, you can keep that one, too." He nodded at Reuben.

Reuben said, "I don't get it. Why would Dame Charlotte's murderer want you dead?"

Simon smiled. "If you are not the killer, then the killer will be Saxe-Ogilvy's bastard, who must still be alive. We must find out which one that is."

They nodded. They all knew that old story.

After a moment Reuben said, "That's why the lady married you, right?"

Simon said, "Yes. To make sure the plantation would not go to a bastard but to me."

Zoe said, "Well, but your plan's silly. Do you really think the murderer's going to step right up and confess?" She laughed. "In your dreams."

Reuben said, "If nobody down there knows who killed her but the murderer himself, Zoe's right—your plan won't work."

Simon said, "Have you a better one?"

"Yeah," Reuben said. He put down the knife and wiped his greasy hands on the swim trunks.

They were all looking at him.

"It looks like every one of the people in Quayle's house that day had some earlier connection to Jamaica."

Zoe said, "I've never been here before in my life."

"Yeah, well . . . And for some reason they've all been brought together again. Here."

"Weird," Zoe said.

"By whom?" Simon asked.

Reuben shrugged. "Isn't this whole thing a Tony Quayle production? Look, we know the writer and the historian are both Jamaican, so they're accounted for, they live here. Anybody know anything about Nat Reybuhr?"

Several of the men looked at each other with sly little smiles. Eugene said, "He is a battyman."

"A what?"

"He prefer the flavor chocolate."

"Okay," Reuben said, "so the man's gay and he prefers black lovers. And he came here at times in the past, right?"

Nobody said anything.

"Anybody know him back then?"

If anyone did, they weren't saying.

Reuben shrugged. "How about Margarite Barbon?"

Another uncomfortable silence.

"I believe she live here as a girl," William said. "Something bad happen, as I recall."

"Anybody know anything about that?"

William sat with his legs crossed. He tossed a piece of pigskin with hair still on it back in the fire. "I believe she was reh-p," he said softly.

Zoe gasped. "Who raped her?"

"I recall it was schoolboys committed the crime."

Zoe murmured, "My God."

"The boys were very young."

Zoe said, "But old enough."

Reuben looked around the circle of faces, all studiously bent on the fire.

"Anybody know any more about that?"

More uncomfortable silence. He dropped the subject. "Okay, who does that leave?"

"Branwell Kane. Don't leave Kane out," Zoe said.

"Can anybody connect Kane to Jamaica?"

Nobody could.

"What about Tony Quayle?"

"Noel Coward lived here," Simon said. "Maybe they knew each other. Noel Coward had famous visitors."

"When did Coward die?"

"The late seventies."

Zoe said, "Maybe you're right, but so what? And what about me? I'm only here to play Esme."

Simon said, "You are biracial."

Zoe drew herself up. "So?"

"The heir would be biracial."

Reuben said, "All of this tells us nothing, *nada*. But there's something else: Every one of them has an airtight alibi for the time of Charlotte's death, right?"

"That's right," Zoe said.

"Not one of them was alone for a minute during the time she was killed. Each one was vouched for by somebody else."

Simon said, "Go on."

"Yet one of them killed her."

"But how can that be?" William asked.

"It can be," Reuben said, "because two of them are lying."

Simon's eyebrows went up. He nodded. "It would seem so."

"So all we have to do is discover which two have supplied each other with false alibis."

"While you are instructing us," Simon said in a voice cold with sarcasm, "will you tell us how we are to go about that?"

Reuben really didn't like the bridegroom. The man had drowned him, drugged him, bounced him around semiconscious on the hard seat of a Jeep, cut off his beard and thrown it in the fire, and threatened to shoot him.

So he enjoyed looking Simon steadily in the eye and saying, "It's really quite simple."

42

Jane Boll had told the police and the security guards all she knew about Gabriel, but she doubted if, even for that big reward, those people would venture very far into the mountains where they were not welcome and the drums played day and night. But now they had called in the army. Uniforms were everywhere, and she had heard helicopters mentioned. That seemed to be what they were waiting for.

Jane herself had always loved the mountains. She'd come as a girl "from down a country." The mountains were her home, where she'd often returned while her mother was alive.

The verandah where she dozed on her chaise rose serenely above the officious comings and goings on the grounds. It was a lovely morning and her dreams were lit by tumbling waters and bushes heady with the smell of flowers. So she didn't see the taxi from the airport as it circled slowly, stopped by uniformed guards natty in their blue shorts and tunics, and glanced at absently by film people beset by their multimillion-dollar worries. But she jerked awake when it stopped in front of the house and the macaw woke in the nutmeg tree and voiced his objections to the intrusion.

"Hush up!" she said without looking at the parrot, watching instead a person inside the cab haltingly counting out bills of an unfamiliar currency and handing them to the driver, who reached over his shoulder for the fare.

Then a woman as old as Jane herself got out with difficulty and leaned on a cane looking up at the house while the cab pulled off down the drive.

Jane Boll watched through trailing tendrils of bougainvillea as the visitor pulled out spectacles on a little chain from a silver disk on her shoulder, and settled them on her nose.

Jane gasped and sat up and lowered her feet to the floor. Could it really be?

The phone rang inside but she ignored it, for the visitor was peering up at the porch. When the machine clicked on behind her, it gave her a turn to hear Charlotte commanding the caller to leave a message. Then the old judge's voice much too loud, "Hello hello hello? Are you there, Jane? The doctor and I will leave within the hour, as will others we've been able to contact on such short notice. So if you will, please tell the men to go forward with all appropriate preparations so that things will be in readiness when we arrive."

What was the old fool up to now?

The woman below the steps said, "Hello? Is anybody home?"

Jane Boll planted her cane in front of her and put both hands on it and hoisted herself to her feet. She pulled down the back of her flower-print cotton and limped to the edge of the porch.

The visitor smiled up at her and, aided by the banisters, began to climb, then stopped midway and fanned herself with her handkerchief.

"Jane, is that really you? Do you remember me?"

Jane Boll clamped her lips together to hide the gap in her lower teeth, most of them still her own. Then she brought a hand to her mouth and smiled behind it. "I do," she said, "in spite of the fact we are all putting on years."

43

Tony Quayle got the call from the Turtle Bay police at noon. On top of everything else going on, it was a nuisance to have to go down to the station. He commandeered one of the staff's rental cars and rounded up the cinematographer to drive down the hill with him.

Tanaka asked, "What's going on?"

"I bloody well wish I knew. They say they're holding one of our people."

"Who's missing?"

Tony Quayle grunted. "You mean besides our star?"

"Anything new on that?"

"They were seen in one of the hill villages yesterday afternoon."

"Was the source reliable?"

"As reliable as can be bought. After the village it gets vague."

"No ransom notes?"

"Nothing."

Brian Tanaka laughed. "Don't give up. It'd probably have to come in by mule. Sounds pretty wild up there."

They crept toward the police station through crowds wandering at will across the street, shouting greetings and stopping for conversations. Tony Quayle sat on his horn. "It's always vacation in Turtle Bay."

"Who'd you say the police were holding?"

"Whoever took the message didn't seem to know."

Señor Ribera was incensed. He had suffered many indignities but nothing like this. The cell behind him was crowded with young black men speaking a patois impossible to understand. Trembling with anger, Señor Ribera clutched the bars and peered out into the cellblock, feeling vulnerable with his back to them, but at least able to breathe. Surely someone would come for him.

He knew they were laughing at him behind his back. One moved up beside him and stretched an arm straight out from the shoulder, but still it was some inches over Señor Ribera's head. He whirled out from under the arm. They were laughing, exchanging bills and coins, and the one who collected the most rose and handed roughly half of it to the man who'd stretched his arm over Señor Ribera's head.

They had been betting whether or not he would fit under the fellow's arm! His anger gave way to tears. He turned around and banged his head again and again against the bars. His panama hat fell off.

The man with the arm picked up the hat and said something Señor Ribera couldn't understand, then tapped him on the shoulder and repeated it, but Señor Ribera fled to the corner with his face to the bars.

The man took him by the shoulder and turned him around and thrust some of the bills at him and said in finally understandable words, "You good luck, little man. You have meh-d me money. Take some for yourself."

"I don't want your filthy money!"

The door to the cellblock opened, and there with the jailer stood Tony Quayle and the cinematographer. At first he was relieved to see them, but then he was overcome with shame. What more could life deal him after this?

"Yes, okay," Quayle said to the policeman. "He's one of ours."

Señor Ribera mustered what dignity he could. When the cell door opened he put on his hat, lifted a haughty chin, stepped into the hall, and said loud enough for his cell-mates to hear, "These people will pay. They'll regret the day they humiliated Rodolfo Ribera." It was an empty threat, but Señor Ribera, like most of the powerless, had come to rely upon impressions of the moment.

44

The Jeep stopped briefly at a village where Zoe was greeted warmly. She hadn't been left behind in the Cockpits. She was necessary to Reuben's plot. Eugene had loaned Reuben an old tweed vest. He had on only the vest and the swim trunks, but still he was sweating. His script was about to go into production, and though he'd claimed it was simple, in the light of day he knew there was only an off chance it would work.

He was amazed and distracted by the changes of scenery on the trip down the mountain—broad meadows in the lap of hills, then fields of coffee plants, then scattered low palm and palmetto, finally plantations of cane, and rain-forest jungle, and, as the Jeep descended, over the tops of the trees the blue Caribbean. He'd like to try painting it.

They encountered a rudimentary road and the Jeep sped up and finally entered the grounds of the plantation by a neglected farm-equipment road. Finally Simon, who was driving, pulled off and told them to get out. He ran headlong into a clump of bitterbush, and they tore at vines and branches and heaped them on the Jeep's rear end till it was hidden. Then the five of them—Simon, Reuben, Eugene, Zoe, and Gabriel—huddled together behind a cluster of gumbo-limbo trees while a patrol passed on its way up the mountain.

"Christ," Simon said, "they've called in the army!"

When the rattle of equipment and muttering voices had faded, they made their way through the openness of the woods where the spice trees grew, spreading out, creeping tree to tree, for the slender trunks of the pimentos were not much protection. In the tangled vines at the edge of the lawn, they waited while soldiers passed not ten feet away with rifles on slings over their shoulders.

Simon whispered sinking to one knee, "it's like an armed camp."

"Too late to worry," Reuben said.

"You can say that!" Simon whispered. "If they get hold of me they could extradite me to the Steh-tes and try me for murder."

"What about me?" Gabriel hissed. "They'll put me in prison for stealin the girl."

And if they get hold of me, Reuben thought, I'm in contempt of court for jumping bail. He didn't think they'd send anybody to Jamaica after him unless they brought a murder charge. And if they did that, he liked the old vest and the swim trunks, he liked the island, and after high dry Santa Fe he found he even liked to sweat. He'd never go back to jail. Though the treatment was decent and the food okay, it did something to your self-respect to be locked up like that. No, he'd stay where he was. He'd let his hair grow, and his beard. He'd learn to carve birds and turtles. He would stay in Jamaica, a beach bum, like something out of Conrad, an outcast of the islands.

But not time yet to think of that. He took Gabriel's arm. "Okay, go!"

He hoped Simon was right, that big as he was, Gabriel could will himself invisible. They retreated into the bush to wait. After an interminable time, while uniformed men passed on the trail to the mountain, Gabriel returned.

"They all there but the boss and the little man. I couldn't find them nowhere."

Tony Quayle and Señor Ribera. Reuben stroked his bobbed beard. Did that weaken his plan? No.

"What *about* Tony Quayle anyway?" Zoe asked.

"If none of the others did it," Reuben said, "that leaves him, we've got him. Right?"

"Oh. I see. Yes, right!"

"Now look," he said, "it all depends on how you play it. Okay?"

Okay, they said.

He looked at Simon and broached a worry that had nagged him. "What happens if it works and we find the killer?"

"That is nothing to you," Simon said. "That is out of your hands."

"Listen," Reuben said, "I won't be a party to any—"

"Let us get on with it."

Reuben hesitated. "Okay," he said. "All right. Zoe?"

Zoe said, "Margarite Barbon."

"Right. Eugene?"

"Nat Reybuhr."

"Okay, Simon?"

"I teh-k the little novelist."

Zoe said, "What about Branwell Kane?"

"Kane's mine," Reuben said.

They crept toward the plantation house. Uniforms were everywhere, but only a few of the movie staff—

mostly technicians milling around or sitting under the trees. It was the hot middle of the day.

"Remember," Reuben said, "*make it real!* Now go!"

45

Nat Reybuhr, stripped to the waist in the heat, had retreated with a newsmagazine to the shade of the makeup trailer's awning. Not that he was interested in the news, but it made him feel closer to home. These delays were getting to him. He imagined he felt worse by the day, that the virus was eating his T cells and bleaching his blood.

He turned to the news of medicine, but dropped the magazine to his lap and was fretfully pinching the bridge of his nose when a smiling black man crept around the end of the trailer, squatted on the ground beside him, and whispered: "Hello, battymahn."

Nat Reybuhr stiffened. He knew the term. He said sharply, "Who are you?"

"Don't battymahn remember?"

The scriptwriter squinted. The man wasn't familiar. But he hadn't been down here in years.

"What do you want?"

Eugene said, "Battymahn, we know your secret."

"I don't know what you're talking about."

"Oh, battymahn he knows."

"Who are you? What do you want?"

217

A smiling Eugene put out his hand and rubbed thumb and fingers together.

The scriptwriter recognized the universal gesture. "I'm not greasing your goddam palm," he said. In Hollywood being gay had not for a long time now been grounds for blackmail. But here in the islands . . . ? He'd heard the Rastafarians were notoriously homophobic.

The smiling man said, "You like to seal our lips, or you want your murderous secret told?"

The scriptwriter rapidly weighed his options.

"How much?"

"All you got, mahn, or I go to the po-lice wid this infor-meh-tion."

Nat Reybuhr's arm shot out and his elbow crooked around Eugene's neck and brought his head close to the chair arm.

"Hey, mahn, what'a divel!"

"What the hell are you talking about? I haven't done anything!"

"Lemme go, mahn! You hurtin me!"

"Listen, you bastard, if you think you can get away with blackmailing me for being gay, think again. I'll break your scrawny neck. A gay man is still a man!"

His head in the vise of Reybuhr's arm, the blackmailer grinned up and said, "Hey, okay, mahn, forget it, okay?"

Nat Reybuhr let go and watched Eugene back off bowing and smiling, and duck out of sight around the corner of the trailer. The scriptwriter was pleased with himself. He stood up and stretched and slapped his leg with the rolled-up magazine. He felt better than he had in days. Suddenly he had an appetite. He walked over to the table laid out for tea and heaped a plate for himself. He'd always been a fighter. He could fight the damn virus.

* * *

Margarite Barbon, in jeans and the sturdiest shoes she could find, was waiting in her trailer for Datrey Moss. The novelist had promised to lead her to the hill village where Zoe and her kidnapper had last been seen, but he was late and she was annoyed. Things were falling rapidly apart. There were scenes she could have been shooting, but the cinematographer had disappeared.

At that moment Datrey Moss was striding toward her up the path in the direction of the cluster of staff trailers when an arm grabbed him around his chest, pinning his arms, and a hand clapped over his mouth. He fought, but he was jerked into the bush and dragged to a clearing surrounded by undergrowth.

The hand and the arm were removed. He spun around and recognized his assailant. "What the hell are you doing, man?"

"I must tell you, you are in danger," Simon whispered, glancing over his shoulder. "Your secret has become known."

The novelist, his eyes never leaving Simon's face, sagged slowly onto a tree stump.

"My God," he said. "How did you find out?" And without waiting for an answer, "Does she know?"

Simon glanced over his shoulder, pretending he'd heard something while he cast around for a reply. He said with what conviction he could muster, "Does it matter?"

"Of course it matters," Datrey Moss said. "The whole thing could fall apart."

These scenes were unscripted and Simon was at a loss.

Datrey Moss stood up and scuffed around with his hands in the pockets of his shorts. He looked up at Simon and his eyes were wet. "Can you believe it? I've found myself wanting her to know. I've thought of telling her myself. She has asked me to take her to one of the hill villages. We'll be going to the mountains alone."

Simon murmured, "The director," wondering what Margarite Barbon had to do with anything.

Datrey Moss said, "But why would anybody want to tell her?" Without waiting for an answer he rushed on. "Part of me would be relieved, but she might walk out on the film and never look at me again."

The writer's face contorted with pain and revulsion. Simon had no idea what this was about, but he had found out all he needed to know. Whatever it was, Datrey Moss's secret had nothing to do with Charlotte's murder. He had backed off to leave the man alone when Moss turned a ravaged face. "All my life I have longed to know her," he said. "But could she ever accept me, a black child of rape?"

Then Simon understood. He wanted to wring Reuben's neck for hatching this harebrained scheme.

Patience had never been one of the director's virtues. But when she heard footsteps approaching she reached for the straw hat she'd bought at the market, determined not to let Datrey see her annoyance.

But it was not Datrey Moss, it was Zoe McNaire who knocked and ducked into the trailer without waiting to be invited.

Margarite Barbon's mouth opened with surprise. "Shhh!" Zoe said.

"Thank God!" the director exclaimed. "How did you escape? Where have you been?"

"Never mind," Zoe said, "I had to talk to you. Look, I have to tell you I know your secret."

The director stared. "What are you talking about?"

A childhood with her enigmatic mother had taught Zoe to read the subtlest of signs. She saw the director's fear and was surprised. They had to check them all out, of course, but she'd never for a moment suspected Margarite Barbon.

Praying she was good enough to fool someone used to recognizing bad acting, she said, "I think you know."

The director looked stricken. She sank onto the couch that curved around the wall under the picture window. Zoe was at a loss, but charm usually worked for her, so instinctively she turned on the charm. She dropped to sit cross-legged on the floor and looked beguilingly up.

When the director drew back, Zoe was sure charm had been a mistake. But then Margarite Barbon sighed and said, "Yes, I always pick up the signals myself. Only . . . I didn't know I'd given out any. Except, perhaps, in avoiding you."

Zoe was confused. She'd known the director didn't like her. But what signals could she be talking about? Certainly nothing to do with Dame Charlotte's murder, that was clear. So she'd discovered what she'd come to discover, but still she was curious.

The director smiled down at her. "You're very perceptive."

Zoe said, "I knew you didn't want me for Esme."

Margarite Barbon nodded. "No, I didn't want to work with you even though I knew you would be the perfect Esme."

Zoe was pleased. "You still think so?"

"After the rape scene yesterday, I am more sure of it than ever."

"That was Kane," Zoe said.

The director nodded. "The man's a bastard, but a brilliant bastard." She leaned forward and put out a tentative hand that stopped short of touching the girl. "It was hard to watch him pawing you."

"Oh, I didn't mind," Zoe said, and laughed. "He's pawed me plenty before."

The director's hand drew back. "I'm sure."

"But no more," Zoe said, picking up the director's revulsion. "I'm through with him."

"You're wise."

"But—" Zoe looked sadly up at the director "—he's not entirely bad, is he? I mean, he has some goodness in him."

Margarite Barbon rose and turned away from Zoe and looked out the curve of the picture window that slightly distorted the view. "I suppose everyone has," she said ironically.

She turned back to the girl. "You don't mind?"

"Mind?" Zoe's forehead wrinkled in bewilderment. "Mind what? I love working with you. I've wanted to ever so long." She rose and backed to the trailer door. "Look, I've got to run." She smiled happily. "I'm so glad you like me. I'm so glad we talked."

When Zoe was gone Margarite Barbon stood with her back to the window and her arms crossed. She was both relieved and disappointed. She'd been mistaken. But what on earth could that little scene have been about?

46

Perdita explained to the housekeeper why she was here, and Jane Boll laid her hand on her breast and allowed herself a moment to recover. Then she called the plantation manager from the field and Matilde from the upstairs bedrooms. "They never tell me what's going on," she grumbled, but she issued directions with a vigor she hadn't felt since the news came of Charlotte's death.

The two made their slow way on their canes along the path down the hill, the same path the bridal couple had climbed not many days before. They stood under the banyan tree to see to the preparations. There were older banyan trees on the grounds, trees that alone made small forests from the tendrils of the parent tree that had fallen from the branches and taken root. But this tree at the foot of the lawns had been kept in check by lawns-keepers, most of its thick vinelike tendrils clipped before they could root themselves, and perhaps for that reason the main trunk had grown enormous and its limbs so wide-spread they could have sheltered a village.

The women wandered in its shade until Jane Boll stopped and planted her cane.

"Here," she said to the plantation manager. "Just here." She pounded the spot again.

Above in the tree the macaw cried, and the lori stole away along the branch, and Perdita looked up in time to escape the bad-tempered bird's response to being wakened. It landed close to Jane Boll, who shook her cane at him. "You evil bird!"

Then the wagon came from the barns, where some of the men had escaped the heat for siesta.

"Humph," Jane said when she saw them coming down the hill in battered straw hats and trousers tied with rope, bringing their shovels with them.

"Come along. We'll leave them to it."

As they made their slow way back to the verandah, guards waved a car in at the gate. Perdita didn't know the men inside. There were two in front, and in back, a distinguished-looking man with a beard, wearing a panama hat.

47

It was Tony Quayle Reuben wanted. It had to have been Quayle who'd accused him and sent him to jail, and Quayle had hung up on him when he called for help. And who but Quayle would have let him serve as scapegoat while they got out of the country? It was Anthony Quayle he wanted, but meanwhile to cover all bases there was Kane.

Gabriel had seen him asleep in a lawn chair under the trees. That made it difficult enough, there in plain view of anybody who happened to be looking. But Kane was not where he was supposed to be.

With the beginnings of panic, he crept around to the trailer with the gold star and Kane's name on the door, and was relieved to find the actor asleep inside with his mouth open.

The man was too broad and long for the little wraparound couch. He'd propped his bare feet on the windowsill.

"Huh? Wha . . . ? Who's there?" He sat up grunting and wiping his eyes with his fists. He looked like a very large infant or a living Buddha. His eyes reluctantly focused. He scowled with recognition.

"What the hell're you doing in Jamaica?"

He reeled upright, leaned over with difficulty, and

rummaged blindly on the floor for his sandals. Pulling one on his toes, he squinted at his visitor. "I thought we left you in Santa Fe."

"You left me in *jail* in Santa Fe," Reuben said.

The actor chuckled. "So we did, so we did."

He put his foot on the floor and rammed it the rest of the way into the sandal. He leaned over grunting to look for the other one but gave up and sat back breathing hard and eyeing Reuben, who leaned over and found the man's other sandal and held it for the other plump foot.

"Thanks," Kane said. His eyes were bloodshot, and his unbuttoned shirt displayed the bulges of his torso. "This heat's obscene," he grumbled. "Why couldn't Quayle shoot these scenes in California?"

He got up and lumbered to the door. The trailer rocked. "Let's get out of this hot box."

He cupped Reuben's shoulder with a heavy paw, shoving him ahead down the flimsy steps made out of what looked like metal lath and making for the captain's chairs under the shade tree. He dropped heavily into one of them. Reuben waited for the canvas to split.

"Sit!" Kane said with a heavy sigh.

Reuben tried to think of his next line.

Kane beat him to it. "Now, what the hell're you doing down here? Come for a vacation, have you?" He chuckled ironically.

"No, I came to warn you. I've found out your secret."

Kane eyed him. Then looking out on the plantation lawns he murmured, "That fucking little bastard."

Reuben was surprised.

Kane sighed and looked back at him with a touch of contempt. "Well well, but you didn't come all the way down here just to tell me that, did you. How much were you hoping to get out of me to keep your mouth shut?"

Before Reuben could come up with an answer, one of the staff cars roared past security check and rushed up the hill and skidded to a stop beside them. Tony Quayle and the cinematographer got out, followed from the back-seat by Señor Ribera. The Spaniard looked from Reuben to Kane.

"We had to run down and get our friend here out of jail," Quayle said. "Can you believe it? He was picked up in the market trying to sell this." He brought out of his pocket an ornate gold necklace studded with big square emeralds, which Reuben recognized. He looked up unbelieving at the little Spaniard, whose face where the beard didn't cover it was rapidly blotching red and white.

Kane said, "Well-well, so you've discovered our little murderer and jewel thief." He laughed.

Señor Ribera went into rigors of rage. "You mastodon!" He pointed a trembling finger at Kane. "I'll protect you no longer! *There's* your murderer. I saw him do it. I was outside the lady's patio door."

Reuben was speechless. Kane?

Kane laughed like he was enjoying himself. "Then why didn't you come forward and tell the police? Who do you think will believe you, you with the lady's necklace?"

Señor Ribera's agitated finger went on pointing. "You smothered her. You threw the oxygen tubes across the room and put the pillow over her face!"

Kane said, "No-no, you lying little bastard, you killed her." Smiling as if he relished the scene. "Your word against mine, you sawed-off thief."

Señor Ribera drew himself up and appealed to them. "He's lying! Don't listen to him! He killed her. When he saw me watching he ripped her jewelry off her neck and pressed it upon me. And thus in a moment of fear and cupidity a man of noble birth sold his honor." Señor Ribera turned away with his head in his hands.

Kane laughed. "No-no, you shimmied up on her bed and smothered her and yanked off her jewels. I saw you stuff most of them in this young fellow's paint box there on the patio."

"I am no murderer," Señor Ribera whimpered.

Kane said, "Who'll believe you?"

Reuben said, "I do."

At that moment a caravan arrived at the gates. They turned to see them swing open and admit a black limousine followed by a silver hearse and several automobiles. The procession moved at a sombre pace toward the banyan tree.

Kane said, "Well-well, the lady arrives. I've been expecting her."

The limousine pulled slowly past the tree and stopped. The doors opened and a plump black man with judicial presence stepped out, followed by a thin white man gray of visage. They waited together while the hearse came to a stop under the spreading branches. The back doors swung open and a clergyman in a lacy white surplice over his black cassock stepped out clutching a prayer book.

A crowd of plantation women rounded the house with arms full of flowers, followed at an interval by men emerging raggedly from the bush in their work clothes.

And—Reuben couldn't believe it—slowly descending the verandah steps came Perdita Waldheimer arm-in-arm with a gaunt black woman on a cane. Leaning together for support, the two made their slow way down the path to join the gathering under the banyan tree.

Kane said, "Well, well, I suppose we must attend."

Puzzled and curious, Reuben, the cinematographer, the Spaniard, and Tony Quayle followed the actor lumbering down the hill.

They stood together behind the mourners while the clergyman eulogized Dame Charlotte at length, then shook holy water on the burled mahogany coffin. Workmen leaned their shovels against the banyan tree and stepped forward to lower the casket.

But then Simon broke through the crowd. "Hold on. Wey-t."

48

At the sound of his voice, the macaw dropped out of the foliage and landed beside the grave and, when Simon stepped toward the head, waddled after him.

Impressive in spite of the rumpled chinos and soiled white shirt, Simon ignored the movie people but nodded to the old judge and the doctor. He stood silent for a moment at the head of the grave as if collecting himself. Then he spoke to the crowd of plantation people. "We know Charlotte had a plan!"

They murmured, "We know it!"

"Charlotte's plan was, divide up the plan-*teh*-tion and give it to you who have worked it all your lives."

Heads nodded. "That what she say!"

"But Charlotte lies dead in her coffin and now the plantation belongs to me."

"That right!" they agreed.

"And I tell you now, I will never do what Charlotte say!"

A murmur began and escalated. Some of the workmen pushed their way through the women and stood looking defiantly at Simon.

He put up a hand and slowly they quieted. "I divide up this plantation in little bitty plots, pretty soon the trees be gone to firewood and the ground wore out with kitchen gardens."

A man cried out, "She promise the land to us!"

Simon nodded. "Your part be a little plot big enough to bury you in."

"You s'pose do what she say!"

He said, "Hush! Listen to me. Who knows how to work this land?"

"We knows!"

"Who knows how to grow cane and coffee and harvest the spices?"

"We knows how!"

"All right then. Here's what we're going to do, we're going to leave the plan-*teh*-tion all in one piece, leave it like it is!"

Women shook their heads and some of the men raised fists. Voices cried out:

"She don't want that!"

"She give it to us!"

"Right. But none of your little plots. I won't have it. We're going to have a *corporation*!"

Some of the men moved closer, jostling for place. One, in a little tweed cap Reuben recognized from the Cockpits, shouted, "Don't want no corporation!"

"Oh yes, George, you do. You know how much money this plan-*teh*-tion takes in?"

"Lot of money," they cried.

"Right. And you're the owners! Every one of you's a shareholder in the Turtle Bay Corporation. All the wealth this plan-*teh*-tion earns, it goes to you, and to your children and your children's children when you are dead. The plan-*teh*-tion stays intact! I won't let it be cut up in little plots and worn out with goats and chickens."

There were still objecting voices.

Eugene cried, "Listen to Simon! Simon smaht! Charlotte send him to school! He learn him all about running a corpor-*eh*-tion. Look at Simon, you looking at chairman of the board."

A scattering of laughter. The murmurs thinned. George in the little tweed cap stood stubbornly with his arms crossed, but he was listening.

Simon looked at him. "You want to talk, we'll talk some more. But now let's bury Charlotte. Come on, crowd in closer." He spread his arms and waved them in. "Let's do her some sankeys."

They quieted and looked at each other. The silence grew. Then Jane Boll in her high, thin, wavering soprano tracked out a line. "When the sun of your life has gone down . . ."

A few timid female voices picked it up, repeated it, and moved the hymn along. "And the clouds in the west turn to gold."

A few hands began raggedly clapping. Then the singing gained momentum, bodies started swaying. The volume rose as more voices joined till a weaving, clapping, singing procession moved toward the grave under the banyan tree. The macaw, alarmed, waddled closer to Simon and hopped on his foot. Simon leaned down and picked up the bird and put it on his shoulder.

"Come on, everybody!" he cried. "Come dress our sister in flowers!" He held out his arms and gathered the people in.

The singing grew loud, the gestures broad. When the hymn ended a woman tracked out another line. "There is much work to do, there's work on ev'ry hand, Hark the cry for help come ringin through the land."

The weaving, clapping procession passed alongside the grave and the mound of flowers rose higher and higher on the coffin. The singing swelled, and the outraged macaw flew off Simon's shoulder and landed in a breadfruit tree, a scarlet flower among the bright green fruit.

A rich contralto soared. "I will meet you in the morning, by the bright riverside."

"When all sorrow has drifted away . . ."

Reuben moved up beside Perdita.

"I see you found Simon," she said.

Actually, it was Simon who'd found him, but he let it go. "I've found out who killed your friend," he said.

But Perdita was pointing with her cane out to where the sun descending laid a path of pounded copper toward them across the water.

Reuben nodded. It was impressive.

Then Jane Boll again, in her high wavering soprano, "Sow-ing in the morn-ing!"

"Sow-ing seeds of kindness, Sow-ing in the noontide and the dew-y eve . . ." The weaving gesturing choir sowed the grave with flowers as it danced past.

When the service was over and the mourners gone, Reuben stayed behind to tell Simon what he knew. But though the workmen with shovels waited a little way off, Simon remained at the head of the grave with his head bowed. Then he touched his fingers to his lips and laid them briefly on the coffin. Moved, Reuben turned away.

49

Simon had called them together in the plantation house. To get their attention he reached behind him and hit a chord on Charlotte's grand piano that was always out of tune because of the humidity. They quieted and looked at him.

"Most of you in this room think I murdered Charlotte Saxe-Ogilvy," he said.

Gabriel and Eugene were on the verandah looking in at the windows. And Margarite Barbon, who wouldn't venture again into the living room, leaned with her arms crossed in the doorway, Datrey Moss standing solicitously beside her.

"But two of you know I did not."

Sitting on the floor with her back to Perdita on the sofa, Zoe muttered to Reuben, "And some of us know some others who didn't."

Simon gave her a look and she shut up.

"What're we doing here?" Tony Quayle wanted to know. "We're behind schedule. With all due respect, now that we have Zoe back we need to be filming." He glanced at the director, who, however, didn't return his look.

"Not till we flush out a murderer," Simon said.

Reuben was sitting beside Perdita. "Look, Blakemore, I tell you I know who—"

But Perdita interrupted. "*Three* of us."

Everybody looked at her and she flushed. "*Three* of us know you didn't kill Charlotte," she said. "I know because I—"

"Right," Simon broke in impatiently, "because you know me, Perdita, and you know I'm no murderer. But two of you know I'm innocent because you know who the killer is."

"No, that's not what I meant," Perdita said, "though what you say is true—I do know you and—"

But Reuben broke in. "*I know* who the killer is, if you'll just—"

Branwell Kane said, "So do I. It was that little runt of a Spaniard over there." He pointed.

Señor Ribera sputtered, "I did not, and you know very well that I did not." He dropped his head. "I am innocent of murder though I am only too guilty of the other thing." His voice had dropped to a whisper.

Tony Quayle said with distaste, "Apparently, señor, it was you who ripped off the woman's jewels."

"I took them, I didn't rip them off," the little man muttered, looking at no one. Then his eyes blazed at Branwell Kane. "*He's the one!* I saw him do it!"

Kane laughed. "Wiggle out of it if you can, you little runt."

Reuben said, "The two of you lied to give each other alibis, but it was you, Kane, who killed her."

Kane turned to him and asked with curiosity, "Why do you say that?"

"You bought Ribera's silence with the lady's jewels. But how would Ribera have bought *your* silence?"

Kane nodded, chuckling. "That's very clever."

Simon sprang across the room and grabbed the actor by the throat.

Perdita screamed. "Simon, don't! He didn't kill Charlotte!"

Simon looked around distractedly. The actor struggling for breath groped at Simon's hands.

"Nobody killed Charlotte!" Perdita said. "Charlotte died of heart failure!"

Jane Boll alone was nodding. "Poor girl," she muttered.

Reuben leapt across the room and pried Simon's hands loose. Simon didn't seem to notice. "What do you mean, heart failure!"

"Well," Perdita said, and touched her nose with her handkerchief, "the lieutenant—that's Lieutenant Gonzales of the Santa Fe Police—he explained it to me. You see, something kept bothering him about a pillow the murderer was supposed to have used to smother her. And finally he got it out from wherever they keep the evidence and studied it again. Once he thought he understood, he asked the medical examiner to look at—at Charlotte's eyes. And that's how he verified his suspicions."

She looked around, but they still waited. She patted Jane Boll's arm. "You and I know, Jane, that Charlotte was vain. And as she got older she liked to paint her face. And that pillow held her image. In the makeup, you see."

Jane Boll chuckled. "Charlotte always at that mirror."

Perdita murmured, "When she was young she was very beautiful."

Kane laughed. "That old colonialist was made up like a tart."

"She was no colonialist," Perdita said sternly.

"Of course she was! She owned this place, didn't she? And worked these people like slaves."

Perdita shook her head. "That's not true. As long as her husband was alive—and he only recently died—Charlotte could merely plan what to do with the plantation if she outlived him. She sent Simon off to be educated, all the while the two of them writing back and forth, making plans for the plantation's future."

"And fighting over them," Simon said.

"As her senile husband lived on and Charlotte's health worsened, she tried to adopt Simon but his mother wouldn't hear of it. And always she'd feared the appearance of another heir. Charlotte had been very jealous of her husband's women. She was superstitious about that old story, though years had passed and nobody believed it anymore. So when Saxe-Ogilvy died, to protect the plan—by assuring, you see, that Simon would be the heir and carry it out—she quickly married the boy."

Simon said, "That is what happened."

Margarite Barbon said from the doorway, "Do you mean to say somebody 'smothered' a dead woman?"

"That's right," Perdita said. "That's what the lieutenant said."

"But why?"

"That's the only thing the lieutenant couldn't tell me, because he didn't know. But he assured me there was no murder, only the intent to make her death *look* like murder. It was that pillow—and Charlotte's eyes. Whenever he thought of that pillow, he saw her *looking back at him*, don't you see."

They didn't.

She looked hastily down at her lap to hide her horror.

"Well, he saw Charlotte's body the day she died, and later he saw all her cosmetic things on the dresser in my house. Charlotte wore eye shadow, lots of it. Purple," she added so low they hardly heard. "And there was eye shadow on her face as she lay there dead, and eye shadow on her dresser in my guest room. But there was no eye shadow on that pillow."

She looked around, encouraging them to see. Still they didn't. She drew a breath.

"Well, the lieutenant finally put it all together. Charlotte's eyes had to have been *open* when that pillow came down on her face. The lieutenant—such a clever man— the lieutenant said the natural reaction of a person awake, upon seeing a pillow coming down on her face, would be to close her eyes—and also to cry out, of course, and nobody heard anything. And a person asleep would already have her eyes closed. So, you see, he finally realized—from the makeup, don't you know, and from the way Charlotte kept staring at him from that pillow—that her eyes were *open* when the pillow descended. Charlotte was already dead."

They were silent, taking it in.

"And, oh yes, the medical examiner." She was rushing now to get it told. "Charlotte was on a lot of medication, so the medical examiner had to wait for the toxicology report before he could rule out other causes . . . for everybody *finally* dies of heart failure. But they found nothing to suggest that she'd died of anything else.

"And . . ." She looked down at the handkerchief she was tearing in her lap. "And of course there was the other thing." She paused and dabbed her lips. Zoe at her feet reached up and patted her hand.

"Oh, I'm all right," Perdita said, "it's just that . . . to verify his suspicions the lieutenant asked the medical examiner to have a look at Charlotte's eyes. And as he suspected, the corneas were scratched—by that pillow someone had screwed down over her face."

She looked reprovingly at Kane, who cleared his throat, rose clumsily to his feet, and tried hiking his belt up over his stomach. "All right," he said. "So now you know. The lady's buried. Let's bury the rest and get on with the shooting. I can't stand the heat of this place much longer."

"Just wait a damn minute!" Reuben said. "Why would you do a thing like that? What was your motive?"

Simon moved menacingly to block the door. "You did it to implicate me," he said. "Am I right?"

Kane sighed and nodded. "I knew you'd be the suspect."

"And with Charlotte dead and me in prison, that would get both of us out of the way so someone else could inherit."

"Why should *you* inherit!?" Kane exclaimed, his face engorged with sudden rage. "A pampered, overeducated, light-skinned gigolo! You're a traitor to your race!"

Perdita murmured, "He's no such thing. What an awful thing to say."

Kane tried to move around Simon. "Forget about it. It didn't work. No crime's been committed. Nobody's ever been convicted of smothering a dead woman."

Anthony Quayle said, "But *why*?"

Kane said with a fake little laugh that convinced Reuben he was acting, "I'm familiar with your need for excitement, Tony. It's the only thing makes a dead man like you feel alive." He looked down at the producer still sitting there with his legs crossed. "I thought I'd serve you up a murder, a corpse, the police, right in your own house. Why not? I found it amusing."

Reuben said, "They accused me! I went to jail!"

"Yes, well, and I bailed you out. If you want to shout at somebody, shout at that little runt."

Señor Ribera was bent with shame in one of the wicker chairs.

"Ask him why he put the jewelry in your paint box. I'll tell you why. He couldn't cram all of it in his hollow-headed cane. Only room in there for a pint of Scotch, eh, Shorty, when you can cadge it out of somebody's decanter. He jammed the emeralds in there and hid the rest in your paint box before they could find it on him. In his handkerchief! What's your name, Ribera? Roberto? Reynaldo? Rodolfo? You must have the same initials," he said to Reuben. "So—your paint box, your initials, what were the police to think? I doubt the little bastard meant to implicate you. He probably thought he'd get all the necklaces back, only you made off with that paint box before he had a chance."

Señor Ribera murmured, "Why do you hate me so?"

Kane looked at him with contempt. "Their legacy of corruption still cripples every country the Spanish claimed in the Americas!"

Tony Quayle turned to Reuben. "My dear chap, I *am* sorry. How was I to know?"

Reuben wouldn't look at him.

Simon turned his back on the room and leaned on the piano, shaking his head in disbelief.

Zoe stood up abruptly. "For God's sake, let me out of here. You're despicable, Kane."

Kane chuckled. "Yes yes, my dear, I know."

Disgusted, Margarite Barbon followed her out, Datrey Moss hurrying at her heels. "Madam, I must speak to you in private."

"Yes, what is it?" But she kept going, glad to distance herself from this house.

"A few questions about the script," the young man murmured, speaking hastily at her side.

"The script's fine. Nothing's wrong now with the script. I love the script. I love the novel. You're very gifted. I'm sure your mother's proud of you. Now leave me alone."

Datrey Moss stopped in his tracks and looked after her as she rushed away. "Dear lady," he whispered, "may you prove to be right."

Nat Reybuhr, who had followed them out, watched the scene with interest, then sauntered off down the lawn.

After so much stimulation Perdita needed a rest. Jane Boll had Matilde, who was pouting at Simon's lack of attention, show her to the bedroom upstairs where they'd taken her things. Then she said indignantly, "Why you give that girl *her* brooch!?"

And Simon said, "Not now, Jane, not now."

And Jane Boll humphed out of the room. The only ones left were Simon, Reuben, Tony Quayle, and Kane.

"I think you're lying, Kane," Simon said.

Kane dropped heavily on the sofa and looked up at him.

Tony Quayle said, "He's right, Kane. Even you wouldn't perform such a grotesque act for its entertainment value."

Reuben said, "He's too old to be the bastard heir."

Tony Quayle sighed as if one more surprise was one too many. "What bastard heir?"

Simon stood over Kane with his hands on his hips. "Whatever your game, Dame Charlotte's will is airtight."

Kane sighed with resignation and his lips puckered and bubbled like an infant's. "Her bedroom door was cracked open, I saw the old lady lying there obviously dead, I acted on impulse. I did what I did to make it look like murder and implicate you because your marriage disgusted me. But the painter is right, I'm not the heir."

He paused with his actor's sense of timing.

"Twenty years ago I was sleeping with a woman who'd been born in the Caymans of a Jamaican mother. She told me the story—she thought a film could be made of it. It went like this. Her mother, pregnant with her at the time, had left Jamaica in exchange for having her unborn child acknowledged and legitimized by the white father, a lecherous Brit named Saxe-Ogilvy. The woman wanted the child's future insured. She was happy to leave Jamaica—her part of the bargain—because she was afraid. The man was ruthless.

"But once out at sea, the fellow sailing the boat—it turned out he was a former officer in Saxe-Ogilvy's regiment—the man tried to put her overboard."

"Quite a story!" Quayle said.

"Yes, well, but he didn't manage to get rid of her—along with her child and the legal document—because she killed him."

Quayle exclaimed.

"Yes, well, don't forget, Tony, this is no motion picture. She managed to hit him over the head with the fire extinguisher. She didn't know if he was dead and she didn't wait to find out. She tied weights to him and shoved him overboard."

"God," Reuben breathed.

"Heaven only knows how she managed to sail the boat to the Caymans. She was very young, and very pregnant. Once in sight of land she bashed holes in the hull with the fire hatchet and put out the anchor. She wrapped her document in oilskin and swam off and watched it sink. End of story."

Quayle said, "I can quite see it as a film."

"She worked as a domestic in the Caymans till the child was born. The story tempted me to sign on for your film, Tony. I was curious about Turtle Bay Plantation, whose owner I'd come to despise."

"Charlotte was no monster," Simon said. "It was Saxe-Ogilvy."

"She stayed with him, didn't she? She didn't give up the rich life."

"She did a lot of good here," Simon said. "And dead she'll do more."

"Well, so you say. Understandable you'd defend her. You got enough out of her. Everything here is yours."

"Insult me all you like," Simon said. "But insult that lady I'll bloody well smear your face on the floor."

Quayle said, "So the heir is actually your ex-mistress somewhere in California."

Kane smiled. "The pregnant woman who escaped the island would now be my age." He laughed. "I haven't had a mistress my age since I was thirty. No, my mistress was the babe in her womb, Saxe-Ogilvy's child."

Reuben nodded. "I get it. You wanted the plantation for her. Is that why you did it?"

Kane waved that aside with a plump hand. "The woman is dying, whittled away by diabetes."

"If she needs money I'll see she gets it," Simon said.

"She doesn't need money. I've taken care of that."

"What, then? You did it out of malice?"

Kane looked down and plucked at the flower print on the cushion beside him. "Call it revenge by proxy." Grunting with effort, he struggled to his feet.

He got almost to the door before Tony Quayle said, "It's Zoe, isn't it."

Sweat pouring down his face and neck, hair plastered to his skull, Kane said without turning, "Leave it alone, Quayle."

"You committed this gross act for a girl who hates you?"

Kane steadied himself and moved toward the hall.

Quayle gasped out a laugh of illumination. "Why didn't you let her have your child, Kane? She's a healthy kid, she wanted it, and heaven knows you've fathered bastards before and gotten away with it."

"She was underage," Kane said, still not turning.

"Who was to know?"

"Her mother threatened to take me to court with this DNA thing!"

Quayle laughed triumphantly. "How long ago was it that you slept with Saxe-Ogilvy's bastard, the child born in the Caymans? And let's see now, how old was Zoe when you got her pregnant?"

Kane groped for the doorframe.

"I'm right! Look at him! Saxe-Ogilvy's bastard is Zoe's mother! When she dies, Zoe will be the heir! And you found out from your ex-mistress, the one with diabetes, that Zoe's *your daughter*! Was *that* the DNA the outraged mother threatened you with?"

Kane dropped in a wicker chair that groaned under his weight. "You bastard," he whispered.

Reuben wanted out. He stood up, hoping to pass unnoticed under the silently turning fan. But Simon said to him softly in a voice laced with irony, "Your plot seems to have worked."

The makeup man bounded up the porch steps. "You in there, Kane? She wants to try a little shoot this afternoon! I'll need you in makeup!"

Kane rose unsteadily and took Reuben's arm for support. They crossed the verandah. Then framed by bougainvillea at the top of the steps, Reuben watched him lumber off, admiring in spite of himself an actor who, taking a little from Oedipus, a little from Lear, out of incest, guilt, and twisted paternal love, could perform such an outrageous act.

Armisted Whatley hurried up the steps and grabbed his arm. "Have you seen Quayle? I must talk to him at once."

Reuben only then realized that Whatley hadn't been inside for the meeting.

"Yeah, sure," he said. "He's inside. He's . . . Here he comes now."

Whatley hurried across the porch and took the producer's arm. "Please, you must come with me. You've got to speak to Datrey. You really must stop the boy."

Reuben sauntered off down the steps. Behind him Whatley was saying, "If he tells her now it could endanger the film. No telling how she'd take it . . . a devastating experience . . . just a girl at the time . . . Catholic, you see, and even though . . . no getting around it, according to the Church she had to give birth. But you must stop him. He must not make himself known, not until . . . the filming . . . perhaps not even then. Because you see . . ."

Quayle said, "My dear fellow, I haven't the faintest idea what you're talking about."

But shaken by revelations too rich for his blood, Reuben thought he did.

50

In Miami flights were grounded by a weather delay. Here at the tail end of the dangerous season, winds off Puerto Rico threatened to reach hurricane force. Except for a group of businessmen wrangling at a table in the corner, and a man in a seersucker suit asleep on one of the sofas, only Reuben, Perdita, and Anthony Quayle occupied the VIP Lounge.

Reuben sprawled on one of the couches and stared out the windows at the wet tarmac where a luggage cart with its curtains whipped by the wind did a U-turn and headed for the terminal in driving rain.

"I say, old chap," Tony Quayle said behind him.

Reuben scowled. Because of this man he still had to show up in court on his trial date to have the charges against him dismissed. Tito had told Perdita, "He's in the system. He'll have to appear."

"Like me to get you anything?" he asked Perdita.

Perdita went on nodding over a magazine he'd got for her at the newsstand.

Tony Quayle tried again. "My dear fellow, I'm ever so sorry for the misunderstanding. I do hope you'll see fit to forgive me. When the officers looked for you and found you gone with all your things, and the apartment cleared out, and then the Porsche . . . Well, I hope you'll come to see why I . . ."

Reuben went on ignoring him. But after a while curiosity prevailed.

"How'd you know about all those people?" he asked. "You always employ your own private eye?"

Quayle moved into his vision to stand with a drink in hand looking out at the wind-driven rain. He sipped.

"Well, actually I'd no idea what I'd set in motion. I didn't know all of it. Not by half. I once at a party overheard Barbon turn down a vacation in Jamaica. She was a little drunk. Said she'd been born there and would never go back. Naturally, I wondered why. As for Whatley and Ribera—" he chuckled and sipped "—I attended a lecture at UCLA while considering this project, and the two of them tore each other apart. I thought they'd make capital consultants. Get both sides of the picture, don't you know."

He turned from the window and looked down at Reuben. "Kane and Zoe? I thought that was a lover's quarrel Kane wanted to patch up. He refused to sign on unless I hired her to play the slave girl."

One hand in the pocket of a suit badly rumpled from the humidity, the other holding the empty glass, he rocked on his feet.

"I'll let you in on a little secret," he said. "Filmmakers are prone to pet theories about what makes a good cast. Goldman wants people he can count on to get along well, people known to like each other. Paynter, on the other hand, prefers people with no history at all, who don't even know each other, on the theory that in the time it takes to complete filming, competition and enmity cannot develop. Well, I think perhaps they're both wrong. I have my own theory. I wanted to try *tension* as the adhesive. It's tension that's needed from start to finish in a film. And to get it I wanted to experiment with people who detest each other. I admit it's a gamble."

Reuben saw the man's excitement and his wish to prolong the exchange, but pretending boredom satisfied some need in him for retaliation. And the more he pretended, the greater Quayle's urgency.

"Let me explain. I once played the villain opposite Bran Kane's hero. We were already, you might say, locked in mortal combat—he'd already beat me out of an Oscar. And that film I made with him was the best acting I'd ever done. He of course won the girl." He chuckled.

A waiter appeared and he held out his glass for another Scotch.

"Believe me, if there's anything I can do to make up for your inconvenience."

Inconvenience. Reuben liked that. He wished they were still in Jamaica. They'd stayed on through yesterday. While Perdita visited with Jane Boll he'd spent the day on the beach with Simon, who'd taken him out to the reef in his uncle's glass-bottom boat, and for the first time in his life he'd snorkled over schools of tropical fish that put his painter's palette to shame. Later, they'd been badly beaten at beach volleyball by a couple of guys from Negril. Zoe had met them when her day's shoot was finished, and they'd gone to a reggae club and danced till Zoe was recognized. While Simon distracted the mob with a round of drinks for everybody, Reuben had whisked her away, back to an exclusive resort up the coast leased for the stars and crew for the duration of their stay in Jamaica. They'd drunk too much rum on the terrace, and she kept kissing him like she was taste-testing.

Wind whipped sheets of rain against the glass, but smiling he saw instead the path of the moon on the water. When Tina came to mind, he thought he might mention going dancing with the star. He regretted his principles wouldn't let him hint what happened next.

A Cuban in a white jacket wheeled in their lunch. Perdita put her magazine aside. They sat together at one small table while Anthony Quayle sat alone at another. The company men had disappeared. The man in the seer-sucker suit slept on.

Lunch was lobster salad, then filet mignon and the works, with champagne and the airline's apologies for the delay. Then the voice over the speaker announced, in those phony tones that bothered him, that the storm had fizzled out and within the hour they'd be on their way.

In spite of everything, he'd really liked Jamaica. And he'd enjoyed Tony Quayle's anxious smiles, the quiet of the VIP Lounge, the lobster and steak and the bubbly. He was going to miss the Porsche, the apartment, the stipend, pool, and view of the mountains. Admit it, he told himself, with a groan that raised Perdita's eyebrows, you could get used to this life.

That was another thing that bothered him.

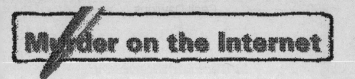
Murder on the Internet

Ballantine mysteries are on the Web!

Read about your favorite Ballantine authors and upcoming books in our monthly electronic newsletter MURDER ON THE INTERNET, at **www.randomhouse.com/BB/MOTI**.

Including:

- ☠What's new in the stores
- ☠Previews of upcoming books for the next three months
- ☠In-depth interviews with mystery authors and publishers
- ☠Calendars of signings and readings for Ballantine mystery authors
- ☠Bibliographies of mystery authors
- ☠Excerpts from new mysteries

To subscribe to MURDER ON THE INTERNET, send an e-mail to **srandol@randomhouse.com** asking to be added to the subscription list. You will receive the next issue as soon as it's available.

Find out more about whodunit! For sample chapters from current and upcoming Ballantine mysteries, visit us at **www.randomhouse.com/BB/mystery**.